I am Harriet Marwood, sir. I saw your advertisement in *The Morning Post* , and I have come to see you personally."

"Ah!" he said. "Ah, excellent! You are the teacher then, the governess."

Miss Marwood bowed.

"And—ummm—let me see. You have—you have your certificates , ma'am?"

"I have, sir," said the young woman, suppressing a faint smile. She opened her reticule and drew out a sheaf of parchments.

"Splendid," he muttered. "Absolutely splendid. Ummm." He tugged at his mustache. "And now—as to this matter of—of firmness. You understand what's needed, of course?"

Miss Marwood's eyes flickered slightly, and she compressed her lips for an instant before replying, "Certainly." She paused again. "But I should like to know, sir, the particular reason for the regime of correction. Is it idleness, want of application, or is it a habit of some kind?" Her fine eyes fixed inquiringly on his.

Masquerade
Books

Date: 3/2/21   Time: 4:43 pm
Auburn Town Pizza   508-832-5210

To Go   #69

Large 2 Item Pizza $14.45
    Ham
    Pineapple
Subtotal $14.45
Tax $1.01
Total $15.46

Cash $15.46

Balance Due $0.00

Thank you, come back again!

THE
ENGLISH
GOVERNESS

ANONYMOUS

MASQUERADE BOOKS, INC.
801 SECOND AVENUE
NEW YORK, N.Y. 10017

The English Governess
Copyright © 1990 by Masquerade Books
All Rights Reserved

First Masquerade Edition 1990

Second Printing January 1996

ISBN 1-56333-373-2

Cover Photograph © 1996 by Robert Chouraqui

Cover Design by Dayna Navaro

Manufactured in the United States of America
Published by Masquerade Books, Inc.
801 Second Avenue
New York, N.Y. 10017

"Indeed it seems to want no demonstration
The best thing for a boy is flagellation:
The doctrine need not exercise our wit;
'Tis shown by Reason, and by Holy Writ,
All education is summed up by this:
A good sound whipping never comes amiss."

—*Coleman: Squire Hardman.*

PART ONE
CHAPTER ONE

On London's Great Portland Street, not far from All Souls Church, there is a row of gloomy mansions that have not changed appreciably in the last half century. The same tall narrow windows, the same grey and sombre stone (only darker now from the encrustations of fifty years' soot), the same recessed and pillared doorways. They confront the passer-by as in the final quarter of the last century, and the same impression of sternness and secrecy prevails. Who lives there now? That does not matter. The neighborhood is still respectable, but the whole street has an air of exhaustion, of having played out its part, of being, in every sense of the word, finished.

This impression seems to become intensified to the south of the great church, where stands the row of houses mentioned. They seem, somehow, the saddest in the world. Can it be that their sadness somehow springs from a mysterious discrepancy between the vigorous, blazing life they once contained and the embers and ashes they now suggest? It may well be. These houses have doubtless seen better days. Happiness, you would say, had at one time made her home here, and has now gone elsewhere.

Happiness, yes: and more than that, romance. For here, more than sixty years ago, in that great gloomy house opposite—the third past Langham Street, to be precise—there blossomed the romance of Richard Lovel and Harriet Marwood. It was a story so bizarre in its beginnings, so fraught with suffering in its outcome, that the old house, which witnessed its birth and infancy, might well look melancholy with the despair of seeing such a story ever matched.

And it is true that such loves as Richard and Harriet's have gone out of style, like the habits, manners and costumes of the past: laws and customs change, carrying away the very conditions of such a romance, its climate and source. So now these old love stories can only serve us as fictions, as dreams maybe, of something gone forever. Of an ideal towards which we can yearn but not follow. Of which we can enjoy with the added knowledge, at once sweet yet full of boundless regret, that such things can never happen again. For there are loves that are impossible in the world as it is these days.

In the year 188-, when this story begins, the Lovel family, one of the oldest in the county of Hampshire, had for two generations its seat in the big house on Great Portland Street. The move had been made in the late 'fifties by Mr. Richard Lovel, the first of his line to distinguish himself in any way other than by exercise of an enlightened self-interest and an adherence to principles of the most orthodox conservatism. The gentleman had speculated in railway shares to such advantage that within ten years, by the employment of methods into which we need not enquire too closely, he had realized the comfortable fortune of nearly £50,000. This sum had been enough for his wants. He had then sold most of his patrimony near Christchurch, reserving only a cottage built on the site of the earliest Lovel holding, and settled for good on Great Portland Street. There, as if the transplantation had not agreed with him, he died within three years.

He had had only one child, a son remarkable during his youth for the elegance of his manners and his habit of dissipation, as well as the size and vigor of his virile member, which was almost a byword in the demimonde of dancers, courtesans, and smart masseuses he frequented. But these distinctions had been accompanied by considerable shrewdness in business affairs.

On his father's sudden death young Arthur Lovel, without curtailing either his pleasures or his life in society, soon settled into the life of business. He proved so adept that the family fortune increased rapidly under his hands. At the age of thirty, he had married the Lady Edith Belsize, the fourth daughter of an impoverished peer who was delighted with Arthur's waiver of the question of settlements. He had undertaken this marriage for two reasons that seemed highly sensible to him—the beauty and the title of the young woman.

He received no more than these. His wife never loved him. Indeed it is doubtful if the emotion of love could ever have found a place in the bosom of that cold but beautiful girl, while the curious sexu-

9

al behavior of her husband did nothing to attach him to her. Arthur Lovel, assured that she at least would fall in love with nobody else, had returned to his business and his pleasures with an easy mind. The fruit of this unhappy union was an only son.

Richard Belsize Lovel was but a lad when his mother died. He was at this time, when we first make his acquaintance, a rather insignificant boy, small for his age, shy, of a reserved disposition and a sweet and even temper. Outwardly, he was timid and passive; even the delicate beauty inherited from his mother recalled the frail and affected grace of a girl. At school his comrades at first called him Sissy, Sissy Lovel. He had blushed at the nickname, but made no attempt to deserve any other.

But it was not long before his most striking trait emerged. It was an inordinate sensuality of both mind and body; and it earned him the only distinction he enjoyed among his schoolmates: He was then admiringly called Smuggy: Smuggy Lovel, in recognition of his sexual prowess at the nightly sessions of onanism in the dormitory, where he displayed a singular felicity at producing repeated erections and orgasms. The distinction was short-lived, however. His proficiency in this field led to his being publicly expelled from the school only a few months after his mother's death.

For the rest of him, he was far from being stupid. The depth and swiftness of his intelligence, allied to his shyness, sensuality and tendency toward self-effacement, would have combined to assure him—at least in the world's view—a future either full of unhappiness or of a rich and rapturous fantasia. Of him, as of the young Hartley

Coleridge, it might have been said at this time,
Nature will either end thee quite,
Or, lengthening out thy season of delight,
Preserve for thee by individual right
A young lamb's heart among the full-grown flocks.

His father, as we have said, was a man of both business and pleasure. He had never attended closely to his home, much less to Richard's upbringing. The sudden death of Lady Edith and the boy's expulsion from school, left him in a quandary. He had known of his son's solitary habits, which he deprecated strongly, but believing that this was a matter for his wife's attention rather than his own he had forborne any action. The expulsion, however, caused him real concern. He saw the now motherless boy in danger of being permanently branded with the stigma of a shameful and ridiculous habit.

"Good God," he said, "what am I to do with this wretched boy of mine?"

The question was not rhetorical, for the woman he was addressing was his regular mistress, an Irishwoman of great beauty but humble extraction, whose practical good sense he valued quite as much as he did her skill in giving him pleasure. At the moment of his question they were lying on the daybed in the darkened room of her smart flat, and for some time she had been occupied in stroking and sucking his member into a fresh erection after its repeated ejaculations. Now, without ceasing the play of her fingers, she answered her protector.

"I will be a fool then, Arthur, and tell you."

"A fool, Kate?"

"Yes, for I'll be risking having a rival. And yet

11

I'm only a fool for telling you what any fool can tell you. What the boy needs is a woman to look after him at home."

"A woman? In my house? God forbid."

"And why not? One of these respectable women you English have so many of, these governesses I mean—daughters of clergyman and such, right-minded, well-educated, strong-handed young ladies, certificates all in order. I mean one of those women who can take a boy like yours in hand and make a man of him."

Mr. Lovel was silent. He played with the nipple of his mistress' swelling breast with an absent air as she went on.

"Yes, and you must make sure you find one that's prepared to use strong measures, Arthur. The boy needs discipline, you know."

"Eh? You mean that's the way to cure him of this vile habit?"

"I do indeed. There's only one way of breaking the boy of it. It must be fairly flogged out of him. So see you get the right kind of governess, and leave the rest to her."

Mr. Lovel was silent once more for a few moments. Then he nodded briefly, as if to himself, and turned his attention back to the naked woman who was still skillfully masturbating his member. His hands were toying now with her ample buttocks, seeking the anus.

Kate laughed. "You're ready for more buggery now, are you not? Well, and so am I...Come now, I'll suck you again for a bit so you can slip in easily and take your pleasure as you like it."

Mr. Lovel smiled as her warm wet mouth closed around the bulb of his penis, enjoying the complex caress of mobile lips and the rapid titillation of a

strong and expert tongue. His eyes closed luxuriously as one of his mistress' hands massaged his
tense testicles, while the forefinger of the other
swiftly moistened between her own thighs, slipped
into his rectum and tickled the entrance cleverly.
He was already tasting in anticipation the pleasure
of buggering his mistress.

Here we must remark that this rather unusual
taste of Kate's had been developed at an early age
and in a manner that, as her protector often
thought, did great credit to the standards of her
class. For in fact was that her father, a poor work-
ingman who had lost his wife when Kate was barely out of girlhood had, instead of inflicting a step-
mother on the sensitive young girl, sent her to live
with the local parish priest. The priest had regularly taken her to his bed. There, out of consideration
for her virginity, he had regularly sodomized her
most lovingly for several years, thus sowing the
seeds for the passion that was the source of the
mutual pleasure enjoyed by Mr. Lovel and herself.

Now, after bestowing a final vigorous tonguing
to her lover's magnificently erected organ, she rose
and disposed herself to receive it in its favorite
place, stretching her smooth buttocks with her
hands to afford an easier passage to her right
handsome rectum. Mr. Lovel's eyes fixed greedily
for a moment on the light brown wrinkled lips that
were already puffing and contracting rhythmically
in their eagerness to welcome his member. With a
deeply drawn sigh of pleasure he placed its head
against the orifice, and pushing firmly, insinuated
it slowly in the moist and reeking passage.

Kate, with an expert writhing movement of her
loins, already panting with pleasure, let it play in
and out near the entrance to her bowels for the

next few minutes, affording its bulb a veritable massage with the well-developed muscles of her moist sphincter, all the while titillating her own clitoris so as to keep abreast of her lover's pleasure. Gradually, she admitted the stiffly thrusting member deeply and more deeply. Then, quite beside herself with lust, she kept doubling and straightening her spine, panting out all manner of obscenities and encouragements to Arthur. She frigged herself wildly until, as his warm sperm gushed into her bowels, she reached her own crisis and united the spasms of her shaken frame with his.

But in spite of his enjoyment with his mistress, Arthur had not forgotten the problem of his son. A few minutes later he returned to it.

"So I must engage a governess for Richard," he said thoughtfully as Kate tenderly sponged his flaccid member.

"Ah, but be sure you engage the right kind, the flogging kind."

"And how the deuce do I make sure of that?"

"Why, you just insist on firmness. That's the word they will understand. See, when you advertise you must state that it's for a boy who needs a firm hand."

Arthur watched abstractedly as she rolled his soft member delicately in a linen handkerchief to dry it. "A firm hand, eh?" he said with a smile.

"Aye. That will mean the whip, you know. It's well known in their world." She shook scented powder over the now shrunken flesh and patted it in lightly. "Ah, it may be a fool I am in telling you to take a woman into your house, Arthur. But my heart goes out to the poor boy, who is in a fair way to ruin his health and prospects by all that playing with his thing."

Arthur bent forward and kissed his mistress tenderly on the cheek. "Ah, Kate," he murmured, "you need have no worries on the score of losing me to any governess." He smiled. "Is it likely I should ever find a woman as fit for my pleasures as yourself? No, my dear, the woman who likes a member up her rectum is all too rare in this world at any time."

"Well, that's true enough. And I think I know your other tastes and likings in bed better than anyone else will be able to—be she lady, servant, governess or even a common whore like me." And in a sudden burst of affection she pressed her lips to his hand.

Arthur Lovel was deeply touched. "Indeed, Kate my dear," he said, fondling her handsome head, "you are the dearest and wisest whore I have ever had. But come now, let us go back to bed. You shall suck me nicely now, for I think I should like to spend once again, only this time it will be in that lovely mouth of yours which gives me not only such pleasure but such good advice."

CHAPTER TWO

By the end of the following week an avalanche of letters had descended on the sombre mansion on Great Portland Street.

"Devil take that notion I had of advertising," thought Mr. Lovel. "I can't wade through all this."

Nevertheless he had already opened three or four letters and cast his eyes over them rapidly, noting that his prime requirement had been very perfectly grasped. The writers all professed their firmness and left no doubt that they were in fact domestic flagellates possessing a high degree of skill and experience. The very existence of such women was something the worthy man had never suspected.

"How curious," he was thinking, when his valet, Thomas, entered with the announcement that a woman wished to see him.

"A woman? Here?" said Mr. Lovel. He was quite taken aback and immediately suspicious.

18

"What sort of woman is she?" He asked the valet.

"A young sort of woman, sir. What you'd call a young woman, I suppose, sir—only, she's so—so..." Thomas seemed at a total loss for words.

Mr. Lovel, who had long known that Thomas' descriptions partook of a supreme fogginess, reproached himself inwardly for having asked the question, and ordered the lady shown in.

She entered immediately.

Mr. Lovel saw before him a tall young woman in her middle twenties, dressed with quiet elegance. A brunette with a very white skin, she wore her dark, almost black hair in a plain style under her small bonnet, parted from forehead to crown and drawn smoothly back to a heavy chignon at the nape of her strong, graceful neck. Her brow was well-shaped and intellectual. The nose was straight, short and full of energy; the mouth rather wide, with a full underlip. The chin was quite prominent. Everything in her face and pose denoted decision and force. But her glance, reserved, serious, even academic, could not conceal the warm brilliance of her violet-grey eyes. She wore a tight-bodiced gown of plain black silk with a full skirt falling from a bustle and coiling around her feet—a costume that revealed a superb bust, a slender waist, and wide, well-muscled hips.

Mr. Lovel's practiced gaze fixed for an instant on the latter, and pierced the full drapery with ease, appraising the contours beneath it as clearly as if she had been standing nude before him, even to envisioning the center wherein his own desires for a woman were concentrated, the hidden bistre rosebud he knew must be pouting between those magnificent buttocks. But nothing of this showed

in his manner; he had risen and was bowing, waiting
for her to introduce herself.

Her voice was low, well-pitched, very even. "Mr.
Lovel?"

"Yes."

"I am Harriet Marwood, sir."

Mr. Lovel bowed and resumed his interrogatory
air.

"I saw your advertisement in The Morning Post,
and I have come to see you personally."

"Ah!" said the man of business, relaxing and
expelling his breath. "Ah, excellent! You are the
teacher then, the governess."

Miss Marwood bowed.

Mr. Lovel pointed to the desk piled with letters.
"And there, ma'am, are the letters of your competi-
tors. But in point of face, it was an excellent idea to
come in person instead of writing. A capital idea!
And—ummm—let me see. You have—you have
your certificates, ma'am?"

"I have, sir," said the young woman, suppressing
a faint smile. She opened her reticule and drew out
a sheaf of parchments, over which Mr. Lovel cast a
cursory glance before returning them to her.

"Splendid," he muttered. "Absolutely splendid.
Ummm." He tugged at his moustache. "And
now—as to this matter of—of firmness. You understand what's needed, of course?"

Miss Marwood's eyes flickered slightly, and she
compressed her lips for an instant before replying,
"Certainly." She paused again. "But I should like to
know, sir, the particular reason for a regime of
correction. Is it idleness, want of application, a
habit of some kind?" Her fine eyes fixed inquiringly
on his.

Mr. Lovel pursed his lips. "It is—well, it's rather

a delicate matter, Miss Marwood," he said. "But of course you will have to know." In a brief and constrained manner, and with the use of some circumlocution and euphemism, he informed her of his son's proclivities and of his expulsion from school.

Miss Marwood nodded calmly. "This habit cannot yet be inveterate," she said, "seeing he is young. But it may take some time to break him of it."

Mr. Lovel looked at her shrewdly. His embarrassment over the subject was already quite dispelled by her businesslike attitude and air of quiet competence. Suddenly his mind was made up. "Then," he said, "you are prepared to undertake the cure of the boy, as well as his education? You have had experience in these cases?"

"A great deal of experience, Mr. Lovel."

He released his breath. "Well then, it's all settled. Would you like to see him?"

Miss Marwood bowed.

She followed him as he hurried along several gloomy passages and up two flights of stairs, until they reached the large dark library on the ground floor.

"Richard! Ricky!" called Mr. Lovel. "Where are you, my boy? Deuce take the darkness! Ah, there he is. Come here, Richard, and meet your governess."

Richard, who had been lost in a vaguely sensual dream in a dark corner of the great room, rose and came forward uncertainly.

Miss Marwood placed her hands on his shoulders and pushed him gently towards the single great leaded window through which the weak winter daylight filtered. For a few long moments she gazed deeply into his face.

She at once noted his beauty and grace; and she

21

had also marked the downcast gaze, the air of lassitude, and the clear ethereal pallor that denoted only too clearly a slave of constant self-abuse. Now, however, she seemed to be sounding the depths of his character itself, to be discovering the springs of his impulse, to be reading his very soul. The boy's great blue eyes, as if he were hypnotized, could not withdraw from her penetrating gaze. Mr. Lovel watched the examination with a feeling of fascination.

Ah, what would either have thought had they known what was going on behind the white forehead of the young governess? Something like a smile merely curved her full lips for an instant, but did not develop further.

"I am delighted to meet you, Richard," she said. Then, turning to Mr. Lovel, "It will be difficult, sir, but you need have no doubt of my eventual success. When would you wish me to come?"

"Why, as soon as possible, Miss Marwood. The poor boy is bored to death. He does nothing all day long either, and that's bad for him too. He's not naughty otherwise—a little lazy perhaps—idle, independent, you know. But all in all, a good boy." He smiled. "All he needs is firm handling."

Miss Marwood bowed.

"Yes, yes. A firm hand, that's all. And where are you stopping at present, miss?"

"I am at a hotel, sir, on Fitzroy Square. I have been there for almost a week, since I came up from Hampshire."

"Quite, quite. Then, if you will, go and fetch your boxes and things as soon as you can. Ah, so you're from Hampshire, are you? Very interesting. My people come from there too. I've still a small property down there, in fact. Now you must excuse me, I am already due at the office. Au revoir, Miss Marwood. I hope to see you here this evening." He held out his hand.

"I shall be back inside the hour, sir," she said, clasping his fingers firmly. Then she passed her hand, plump and feminine for all its strength, over Richard's cheek, making him tremble and blush to the whites of his eyes.

Mr. Lovel and the governess went out, leaving Richard alone once more in the great dim room. He lit the lamp, chose a book of historical tales, and sat down to read until it was time for dinner. But the words danced before his eyes. His head was so full of Miss Marwood that there was room for nothing else.

He hardly knew whether it had been joy or fear he had felt when her hands were weighing on his shoulders, her fingers caressing his cheek. Ah, that glance that had seemed to pierce to the very depths of his being! For those moments when she had looked into his eyes, he had thought his heart was about to stop beating.

What had she meant to say to him, with that gesture and that smile? A kind of promise, he decided, but whether of good or evil he could not tell. The gaze of those violet-grey eyes had gone through him like a flame, that was all he knew. And now this woman would be living with him. Living with him.

His hand had already strayed downwards and begun to caress the finger of flesh swelling beneath the tight white cloth of his trousers. His eyes closed...

And suddenly it seemed that instead of welcoming this change in his life, he found it a matter of vexation. All his ways and habits would be upset.

No longer would he be able to read, to dream and play when and how he wished. She would be there, giving him orders, interfering with him, interrupting his solitary pleasures...But perhaps she would be easy—and nice, he thought, very nice: then, if he was good, might she not kiss him?

The thought affected him with a sudden weakness, and his penis swelled still further. He had read stories in which beautiful women clasped children in their arms and kissed them. It seemed to him a thing of such unspeakable sweetness that his head swum at the mere idea. Ah, he thought now, his breath quickening, to be held and kissed like that! Already he had opened his trousers and begun stroking his member. As it slowly erected he took his favorite pose, his parted legs twined around the legs of the chair, his feet braced on the rungs, his gaze fixed on his penis itself in a kind of dreamy and almost famous admiration.

This admiration, we must say, was not without a genuine foundation. His puerile organ, which gave no promise of ever attaining the gross proportions of his father's, was already an instrument of extraordinary beauty. Slightly longer and more slender than the average boy's at this age, it stood out firmly from between his legs with a gentle upward curve, an effect of lightness and aspiration that was almost Gothic in its rigid springing line. It formed a harmonious and crowning adjunct to the entire architecture of his body.

The bulb itself, now round, distended and with the franum tautly stretched, was in perfect proportion to the smooth shaft bearing it aloft, with no hint of a common or club-like coarseness. The exquisite double line of the twin lobes swept with the firmness of drapery up from the snugly fitting collar studded with the tiny sensitive spicule of sensation to the sturdy arch of his cleft, where it culminated in a dainty urethral eye shaped like a perfect tear. The color of the bulb itself was a very fine and uniform rose, melted into the paler pink of the fine skin that, now reversed, covered the faintly ridged neck with its soft and almost transparent veil.

It was an instrument made rather to receive pleasure than to give it—the kind that women no sooner see than they wish to take it in their mouths rather than their wombs, to suck it for its own pleasure rather than feel it stirring in them for their own.

Now, under the accustomed ministrations of his fingers, the whole shaft was quivering slightly throughout its length, testifying to the exquisite sensations the tender underside of the franum was receiving, and giving an impression of almost conscious enjoyment. The testicles, drawn up tautly beneath the member itself, were clasped in his left hand, which was kneading them in time with the luxurious rhythmic stroke of the right hand.

Seen thus, he presented a picture full of the most effete and wayward charm. The warm lamplight seemed to make still more touching this splendid self-indulgence of a boy whose languid beauty was immeasurably enhanced by his shameless concentration on the act of pleasure.

Richard was at an age when orgasm comes promptly at call. In less than a minute his member discharged copiously in his hand.

He sat quietly for a few minutes, relishing the pleasure he had given himself, and recalling the image of Miss Marwood's kisses which he had so naively called up to excite himself. Then he remembered that she was not simply a beautiful woman, but a governess. And all at once this word 'governess' distracted him with its suggestion of authority, even despotism, and his thoughts wandered again.

At school he had had a little friend, fresh from home. Like all small boys, they had sucked and fingered each other's genitals at every opportunity. But, in between these fascinating practices, his friend had told fearful stories of his own nursery governess, of her strictness, her savage and instant punishment of the delightful practice of masturbation. These stories of the birch and riding-whip had troubled Richard greatly. Instinctively he feared all women—and since then, governesses most of all.

Well, now he had a governess himself! What would he do if she tried to treat him in the same way? But no, that was out of the question. His friend had been one of the youngest at the school. Richard was no longer a baby and would not be treated like one.

He tried once again to read, but found he could not. He closed the book, walked up and down, and then went to the window and tried to look out into the dark, rain-washed street through the lozenges of multicolored glass—first through an orange one, then a blue, then a red. Through each piece of glass the world outside wore a different aspect.

But this game soon wearied him. He went back into the darkness of his corner, yawned, and looked at the old grandfather clock whose pendulum marked the passage of time with its heavy and monotonous tick. She had said she would return in an hour. But what time was it when she had come? He did not know. All he

knew was that he was awaiting the sight of her
again in a fever of longing. As he began thinking
of her face, her figure, her eyes, the touch of her
hand, the force of his attraction was inevitably
channeled into the slow renewed tumescence of
his flesh. After a while his hand strayed downwards once more to the opening of his trousers...

At the very moment of his second ejaculation
he heard the front door open and the sound of
footsteps ringing in the hall outside, and the clear
vibrant voice of Harriet Marwood giving orders to
the cabman about her luggage. Ah, he had
achieved his orgasm just in time! He adjusted his
clothing swiftly, then went to the door, opened it a
few inches, and peered out. He had a radiant
vision of his governess as she stood in the brightly
lit hall, dressed in a long green mackintosh-cape,
wet and shining, her beautiful face glowing like a
flower within the closely-fitting shirred hood.
Then, to his astonishment, the voice of his father
was heard, and he closed the door again quietly.

"Ah, you are more than prompt, Miss
Marwood!" cried the man of business. "I remembered I had not shown you your room, and I have
waited to do you this courtesy. A thousand par-
dons for my forgetfulness! Yes, hang your cape
here. What a sensible garment you have chosen for
our beastly climate! So smart, so practical...This
way, up this way please. And now I'll leave you
with the boy, eh? Do with him as you see fit. He is
entirely your charge, you are quite at home."

"Thank you, sir. At what time shall I have dinner served?"

"Hmm-mm. Dinner. Oh yes, dinner. My word,
you must arrange with the cook to have it whenever you wish. I never dine at home, you know. And

I lunch in the city nearly every day. Ah, business, business! Never at home," he exclaimed, waving his hands. "Always on the go!"

He disappeared. And Harriet Marwood understood, from the fact of his having waited for her return, how anxious her employer was to delegate his paternal responsibility. She saw that she was, in effect, absolute mistress of the house she had just entered.

CHAPTER THREE

It was half an hour before Harriet descended to the library, where Richard had been awaiting her in all the throes of trepidation and uncertainty. On seeing her he became still more disturbed. She, quite at her ease, approached and tapped him lightly under the chin.

"Well," she said, "what have you been doing since I left?"

He blushed and tried to reply, but an excess of shyness strangled his voice. He was silent.

"Come, are you dumb?"

"No, miss…"

"Well?"

"I—I did nothing at all."

"Nothing at all! But that is unheard of. One must do something."

The last words were accompanied by a gaze of such penetration that he shivered, his eyes involuntarily falling to the region of his genitals for

30

assurance that there were no traces of his indulgence. Harriet's shrewd gaze followed his.

"Come now," she said, with a faint note of mockery in her clear, pleasant voice, "tell me what you have been doing. Begin at the beginning."

She sat down, smoothing out her skirt, and taking his hands in hers she drew him close to her.

"I read—a little," he said. "But…"

"But what?'

"I couldn't read—very much…Then I—I looked out of the window."

"A praiseworthy occupation. And after that?"

He was deeply disturbed, The touch of the young woman's soft hands, the contact of her knees distracted him without his knowing why.

"After that," he mumbled, "I—I did nothing at all…'

"Perfect," said Harriet. "You spend your time well. But you know all that is going to be changed from now on, don't you? We shall begin our studies tomorrow, and you will work hard. Where is your room?"

He led her upstairs. His room was only a few steps from her own. She cast a look of disapproval at the slight untidiness she saw there. "What is that jacket doing on the bed?" she asked, pointing. "Hang it up at once." He obeyed. As he opened his closet she saw his short nightgown hanging on the back of the door, and stepping forward she took it from its hook.

"You will not need this any longer," she announced. "From now on you will sleep without nightclothes."

"Yes, miss," he murmured.

"I shall come and see you here this evening,

when you are in bed," she said. "You say your prayers at bedtime?"

"No, miss…"

"That is disgraceful. We will say them together in future, in my room."

During the hours until dinner, Harriet and Richard talked together in the library. Thus she learned, almost without his being aware of it, not only of the events of her pupil's own life but the immediate history of his family. From a few naive remarks she also learned of Mr. Lovel's addiction to pleasure and of the existence of his mistress.

The hour for dinner arrived. In her room the table was already set. Harriet seated herself with her back to the lamp, her face in shadow. Opposite her, the pale countenance of Richard was in the full light.

Bridget carried in the dishes and set them on the table with a sullen air; but she altered her manner at once on receiving a single glance from Harriet. The glance was so portentous that the old woman understood in that instant what her position in the household was henceforth to be, and she grasped at the same time the fact that she had everything to gain by making herself Harriet's subordinate. Her air at once became respectful, even obsequious.

The soup was served. Richard hungrily took a spoonful and was carrying it to his lips when Harriet leaned forward and stopped his hand. "What are you doing?"

"M-miss—I'm eating!" he stammered.

"And the Grace before meals? You never say Grace?"

"No, miss…"

"You will do so from now on. I shall say the words now, and you will remember them. Tomorrow you will be made say them by yourself."

His head lowered, he listened carefully while she spoke the benediction. Only when she raised her own spoon did he venture to begin eating.

"You have often been in this room?" she said after a while.

"No, miss."

"You will be from now on. When your work is insufficiently done in the daytime, you will make up the arrears here. And when you are to be punished, it will be in this room."

A curious sensation of fear and fascination went through him as he heard these words and saw her beautiful grey eyes fixed on him; but which of these sentiments was uppermost he could not tell. Already he had felt his whole being profoundly disturbed by the personality of his governess, and now with this disturbance there was mixed a feeling of shuddering attraction towards her, a sense of fear at finding himself so absolutely subject to this young woman, and also something else, something indefinable but sweet, almost too sweet...The meal was finished in silence.

Later, when he gained his room, it was with a feeling of having drunk some heady draught that made his head swim deliciously. A peculiar lassitude invaded his whole body. As he undressed, the touch of his clothes slipping over his skin made him shiver, and as soon as he was between the cool sheets a feeling of profound languor made him relax his naked limbs with an exquisite sense of well-being. Instinctively, he turned his face towards his pillow and curled himself into a ball, as if feeling the need for warmth and physical intimacy. Then he closed his eyes, but wasn't able to fall asleep.

He had been in bed scarcely a quarter of an hour

when, very softly, his door was half opened and then closed again. Between these two operations Harriet had slipped into the room without making a sound. She carried a small lamp whose feeble light was further subdued by a heavy shade. On tiptoe she approached the bed and bent over.

The boy was lying on his back now, dozing, his eyes half-closed, lost in a reverie of the one subject that engrossed him—the arrival of Harriet Marwood in the house, and the new life he was entering. But now, thanks to his indulgence of the afternoon, the sensuality of his temperament was no longer aroused by such consideration, and his little penis lay soft and inert between his thighs.

All at once he felt the sheet and coverlet lifted from him; for an instant he felt himself bared to the hips, and then, just a swiftly, the covers were replaced.

He had not time to utter a cry before he recognized his governess. He sat up in bed, shaken by a violent, indefinable fear. But Harriet's hand was laid gently on his head.

"Do not be afraid, Richard," she said softly. "I saw that you were not asleep, and I wished to make sure you were behaving yourself. You were, I see, and all is as it should be. Lie down now, and go to sleep."

He obeyed, stretching himself out, his hand crossed over his chest as if to contain the wild beating of his heart. It was then that he experienced his most intense emotion: Harriet leaned over his bed and kissed him, softly and lingeringly, on the mouth.

"When you have been a good boy during the day," she said, "I will come to you in the evening, like this, to kiss you goodnight…"

He had a moment of daring. As the hand that had slipped beneath his chin was withdrawn, he raised his head suddenly and pressed his lips to it. Then, red as a peony, he turned his head to the wall at his bedside.

"Goodnight, Richard," she said.

And she disappeared.

At this moment Mr. Lovel was also in bed, lying beside his mistress in the rosy light of the bedroom in her flat, where he now spent the greater part of his evenings. He had just withdrawn from the warm embrace of her anal sheath, after spending in it with extraordinary satisfaction.

On this occasion Kate was wearing, for the caprice of her protector, the working dress of the high-class Parisian prostitute of the time—a short transparent chemise over a narrow, tightly laced corset with long black silk stockings tightly gartered at mid-thigh and a pair of leather kid boots with immoderately high heels. In this suggestive costume the whiteness and opulence of her superb body had appeared with such striking and voluptuous effect that she had to withstand two separate amorous assaults in succession before her protector's passions were momentarily sated and she was able to revert to the question of Richard's governess.

"Why," said Mr. Lovel, "I suppose you would call her a handsome woman, Kate, but it's a type that makes no impression on me. Miss Marwood is much too straitlaced, I find."

"That's just as well. But did she strike you as likely to break your boy of that habit of his?"

"I don't know. All I can say is that if anyone can do it, she is the one." He laughed. "She looks like a regular martinet, a holy terror. I don't envy the boy."

"Ah well, it's for his own good. He'll thank us all for it some day." And crooking a handsome leg in its tight black stocking, she coquettishly laid the soft kid of her boot in his lap, counting on it making its effect on his sensuality in due time. "Do you think it will take long?"

"I've no idea, Kate. That's a very handsome boot you have on, my dear. Raise it up will you?"

"There you are," she said, raising her bare thigh. "You like my new boots then? I saw them in Dover Street yesterday and bought them with you in mind."

Mr. Lovel bit the toe of her boot softly, then pressed the soft kid of the upper against his cheek. "Ah, you're a dear girl, Kate. Do you know, I find I don't see half as much of you as I'd like. I've gotten into needing you at the oddest times, my dear—in the middle of the night, first thing in the morning, and so on. Yes, that's right, rub your other boot over my genitals…" He kissed the smartly shod foot before him with slowly mounting emotion.

"My poor Arthur," said Kate. "I had no idea you wanted me so often. It seems that whenever you are here you are fucking my bum or my mouth, and I thought that was enough." She reached for his testicles with a warm hand and began kneading them delicately. "Oh, it's a terrible thing for a man to have an erection in his bed all by himself. It's such a waste."

"And with a mistress like you to remember and think of," he said, gripping her leather-shod foot, "one's almost obliged to masturbate as if one were a damned boy oneself. Listen, Kate, I'll tell you

36

what. You must come and sleep at my house. Now that my poor wife has gone, there can be no complications. You'll come, won't you?"

"My darling Arthur," cried Kate, beside herself with joy, "it's what I have always longed for, didn't you know? Oh, many and many's the long night I've tossed and turned in this lonely bed too, with my arse itching to have your prick in it, my hands empty and craving to be holding your sweet balls, and my throat dry with wanting the taste of your seed. Yes, Arthur, let all that be over and done with, and let me share your bed and your pleasure every night as a man's mistress should."

He took her head between his hands and made the rare gesture of kissing her on the lips. "You shall come tomorrow," he said.

"Now who is the happiest woman in the world!" the good creature cried, jumping up. "For that, I must give you the finest frigging ever a man had! Come, sit down on the stool there now, and put your legs apart."

Arthur rose and sat on the low stool with his legs widely spread, while Kate, drawing up a high chair, sat down facing him. Raising her legs and laying her heels on either side of his testicles, she took his half-awakened member between the sides of her boots and began rolling and rubbing it skillfully against the velvety leather of the uppers. Arthur's eyes shone with pleasure as he followed the slow voluptuous movements of her feet.

"That's a grand way to be frigged when you're in the mood for boot, isn't it?" she said archly.

Arthur looked from her flushed face to his member, which was slowly swelling from the soft friction of the leather, and then to her own widespread thighs that, with her chemise now well tucked up displayed the charming slit of her sex opening and shutting with the rotation of her hips as she kept masturbating him in this ingenious manner.

"Dear Kate," he said, "you can frig a man better with your feet than many a whore can do with her two hands, indeed you can."

"Ah, I'm only too glad I can, since you like it so well. But now you've got me so hot I must frig myself, too." She parted the lips of her vulva, and attacked her swollen clitoris with passionate fingers.

The sight completed the process of her lover's erection. As his member throbbed and pulsated between the churning, kneading feet, he kept his eyes fixed, now on it and now on his mistress' masturbation of herself, until he felt the pleasure of the crisis threading his loins imperiously and discharged his sperm freely into the air. Then, sinking back in happy exhaustion, he followed with critical appreciation the course which Kate was following in the achievement of her own orgasm before his eyes.

CHAPTER FOUR

The next morning at seven o'clock, Harriet, fully dressed, entered her pupil's room again. He was still drowned in slumber, and as on the previous evening she lifted the covers and with a swift glance examined the boy carefully. She at once noted the violent erection of his member, and smiled at this evidence of a temperament so consonant with her plans. Richard had not moved; to waken him she was obliged to shake him by the shoulder. He started up, rubbing his eyes.

"Well, Richard, what do you say?"

"Good—good morning, miss."

"Good morning. It is seven o'clock, the time when you will get up every morning from now on. Come into the bathroom."

He hesitated, all too aware of the distention of his genital.

"Well, I am waiting," she said, her brows knitting in exasperation.

40

"But—but, miss, I'm not—I mean—I mean, my—my…"

"Your what? Come, up with you now at once." With a swift movement, she pulled the covers from his naked body. His hands went instinctively to cover his member. "Oh, so that is what is troubling you! Really, such false modesty is absurd. Get up at once! We are not going to wait for that morning tension to go down." And she turned away impatiently.

He rose in confusion, seized his dressing gown and followed her into the bathroom.

"I have had Bridget draw your bath," said Harriet. "Get into it now."

He looked at her in embarrassment. "Yes, miss…" But he remained motionless, standing before her uncertainly.

"Well, what are you waiting for?"

"I—miss, I shall have to undress…"

"Of course. You do not make a habit of taking a bath in your dressing gown, I hope. Take it off."

He began untying the cord around his waist, hoping she would leave. Then he understood that she meant to be present when he took his bath. He slipped out of the gown and stood nude before her.

She sat down, examining him with her cool, intent glance. This was the first time she had seen him naked, and for all her air of outward calm she was deeply stirred by the beauty of this adolescent body. Her eyes passed appreciatively from point to point, dwelling with connoisseurship now on the plump shoulders, now on the straight slender legs, now on the almost feminine swell of the hips. She fixed her gaze at last on the firm and nervous rondure of buttocks and thighs, and then centering inevitably on the puerile penis. By now soft and pendent, it had withdrawn coyly between his thighs where it formed, with the small tight testicles, a kind of dainty genital triumvirate in a state of modesty and repose. When he was in the water, she drew her chair beside the bathtub.

"I have been entrusted by your father," she said with a smile, "with the task of supervising your whole upbringing. That comprises more than school work, you know. So I shall be here every morning to see that you take your bath, whether you like it or not. Now hurry. Wash yourself thoroughly all over!"

Richard obeyed. He was reminded more and more of his little schoolmate's governess. How far would the resemblance go? And how downright and domineering this woman was! Suddenly disturbed by the thought that he might even now be keeping her waiting, he finished washing himself and was rising to leave the bath when she stopped him.

"What is this?" she said sharply. "Do you not wash your private parts?"

"No, miss—I mean, yes…I thought that—that—"

"You thought you would omit them this morning, I suppose! I told you to wash yourself all over. Kneel down and do so at once, if you please."

He scrambled to his knees in the bath and began soaping his penis with trembling hands. Harriet watched him closely, noting the accustomed gestures with which he was handling himself as he drew back the prepuce and ran his fingers around the head of the shaft itself.

She spoke suddenly. "You play with yourself a good deal, my boy, don't you?"

He gasped and went red as fire, his hands left

their task abruptly. He tried to speak, but could not.

"You need not answer, Richard," she said. She fixed him with the piercing glance of her gray eyes. "I shall have more to say to you on this subject in a few minutes. For the moment, however, you will put your hands behind your head while I finish washing you myself." And rolling up her sleeves she lathered her hands and took hold of his member; in a moment her fingers were firmly palpating its head and neck, while her other hand, passing between his thighs from the rear, grasped his testicles and massaged them briskly.

As her hands plied their double task, the boy's penis, already accustomed to respond instantly to his own manipulations, gradually swelled and stiffened quite independently of his volition. He watched it rising with an indescribable feeling of shame, horror, and pleasure. Harriet, for her part, continued the ablution as if quite unconscious of what was happening. Even when she inserted a smooth finger in the boy's tight anus, the answering throb that elevated his penis to its full height drew no comment from her. Anyone looking at her would have thought she was even ignorant of the very meaning of tumescence. At last she ceased.

"Into the water with you now," she said calmly, "and rinse yourself well...And now get out and dry yourself at once."

The boy obeyed, awkward and embarrassed by the rigid member that was still standing out and swaying before him with an air of arrogance quite out of keeping with his own feelings of shame and confusion. When he finished, Harriet took the towel from him and sat back.

"Come here," she said, drawing him between her knees. "And do not hang your head like that. Yes, look at me. Now, are you listening?"

Her eyes were boring into his. He noted their warm brilliance, so much at variance with the coldness of her tone and the curl of her short upper lip.

"Yes, miss," he whispered.

She settled herself more comfortably in her chair.

"I am going to talk to you very seriously about this habit of yours, Richard. That is because I mean to impress on you the dangers you are running in giving way to it. In the first place, there is the danger to your personality. You are already, I see, quite weak and lacking in character, without this final indulgence of your senses to render you completely spineless. Lacking all will-power, a passive instrument of your own sensuality.

"In the second, there is the danger to your health. Do you know the physical results of constant self-abuse? I do not wish to frighten you, especially when it is not too late for you to turn over a new leaf, but the habit is extremely dangerous. Your present pallor alone is an indication of that.

"And finally there is the moral danger, the danger that this habit may master you to such an extent that you may never be able to find satisfaction in a normal and natural way. Think, Richard: one day you will wish to be married. How will you feel then, facing the woman who you wish to make your wife, if you are already so wedded to a shameful, childish, and weakening habit that you are unable to express your love as God and Nature intended you should?" The governess paused. She had been holding his hands, but now she released them and placed her own hands firmly on his naked hips, drawing him closer to her as she went on. "Those are all reasons for giving up this self-indulgence of yours, and I wish you to think of them constantly from now on. But there is one other reason that is perhaps better than any of those others, Richard, and one that may weigh with you more powerfully than they do." Here she paused again, and suddenly kneading the flesh of his hips with the harsh grip of her strong fingers, she gave him her warm, full-lipped smile. "And that is, Richard, that if I ever catch you playing with yourself I will thrash you to within an inch of your life."

With these words, which fell on him like the blow of a stick, she pushed him away gently and, as if to emphasize her threat, tapped his now subsiding member lightly with her fingers.

"And now, dress yourself, and come to breakfast."

❖ ❖ ❖

As soon as breakfast was over, Harriet and her pupil repaired to the library, now the schoolroom. She pointed out to him where he was to sit, and sat down herself—not opposite but beside him, and in such a way that she could oversee his work at any moment. Thus the first lesson began.

Richard was nervous, awkward and embarrassed by the smallest difficulty. Not only had he lost the habit of study during his long period of idleness, but the presence of Miss Marwood at his side disturbed him strangely. Truly, the effect this young woman had on his imagination and senses was remarkable!

Sitting beside her, he felt the occasional touch of her knee, her hand, her arm. Her bosom pressed his shoulder when she bent over him. At those moments he became giddy. Her cheek kept brushing his, stray locks of her hair tickled his temples, her breath intoxicated him. So great was his disturbance that sometimes his eyes filled with tears and he wished to break into sobs—and all for no reason. Or what could the reason be? Indeed, she was not threatening him now!

The lesson period lasted three hours, and work was resumed after luncheon without any incident to break the monotony of the day.

For a week matters continued thus. Richard, under the awe he felt for Harriet, was working hard and steadily, doing his best to deserve a word of satisfaction and encouragement—even a caress. Whenever she called him to her chair for him to recite a lesson or explain a problem, if his replies were correct she signified approbation with a few light affectionate taps on his loins, such as one might bestow on an infant.

He still wore the short Eton jacket and white trousers he had worn at school, and the touch of her hand, felt through the tight-fitting serge of the latter, had come to excite and disturb him immoderately. At such moments he had a mad impulse to throw himself into her arms, to crush his face against her breast, to huddle himself against her in absolute abandonment of his whole being to her will. It was then that the fever of his senses rose to a height. He felt the blood beating in his head and a sensation of wild and hopeless craving flooded his loins, while the turgescence of his member and the constriction of his clothing affected him with both the shame and the sheer physical pain of a confined and frustrated erection.

Every night she came to see him in bed. She

smoothed his pillow and tucked him in as the tenderest of mothers might have done, then gave him a long kiss on the lips and withdrew, still calm, still apparently cold, leaving him a prey to a thousand confused thoughts and in a kind of ecstasy. And then, alone and naked in his bed, he was left to the torments of his desire and temptation, lying on his back in the dark, his hands pressed tightly to his sides, desperately fighting the impulse to carry out the forbidden self-indulgence that he craved with every nerve in his body and every fibre of his brain. Had it been only the fear of punishment that restrained him, he would have succumbed long before this. But he was bound to this agonizing abstinence by a more imperious taboo, a sense that to give himself this sexual relief would be to commit an act of infidelity to the woman herself. It was often more than an hour before his flesh subsided sufficiently for him to fall asleep, worn out but almost happy in this victory over himself.

By the end of the week he had only one thought, one wish—to be tied always to this woman's apron strings. She was everything to him; he lived only for her. Let us admit it; he was in love with her. And, with the clairvoyance of love, he was aware also of the force and intensity of her own interest in him. Obscurely, he understood that he was a source of frustration for her as well, and this frightened him. He sensed the fact that she was waiting, waiting—but for what? And after a while, obsessed and tormented as he was by the sensuous ordeal he went through twenty times a day, the task of resisting the impulse to give way to his burning desire, he came to believe that it was that very weakness and resumed self-indulgence she was awaiting so she might put her threat of punishment into effect.

This superstition was only half correct. Harriet really desired his abstinence, though for reasons of her own. But it was impossible, after all, for the boy to assess the fact of her mysterious and ardent temperament, to grasp the perverse nature of her love, and the fact that behind her cold and placid demeanor she was inwardly maddened by the desire to begin whipping him.

CHAPTER FIVE

It was a miserable day in mid-February. The pale daylight seemed to be almost expiring, and the grey sky held a hint of snow. Through the schoolroom window the bare branches of the plane-trees in the street could be seen tossing fitfully in the cold wind. Inside, where governess and pupil were sitting at the work table, it was unusually, almost preternaturally quiet. The boy, bent forward in his seat and gripping his pencil, was trying to solve the second of two mathematical problems that had been set to him that afternoon. Harriet let him work on in silence, giving him no assistance. The time for him to present the work to her had already passed, and the boy, beginning to redden with the consciousness of being at fault, was still searching for the solution. The governess surveyed him with an enigmatic look. A small pulse might have been noticed beating in her neck.

"Well, Richard, my boy" she said, her tone meant

50

to chill, "it seems you may have forgotten the time."

"No miss," he replied nervously. "But—but—"

The grey eyes flashed suddenly. "But what? Speak out, sir! I am tired of these absurd hesitations of yours."

He stared at her, his mouth open. Quite unused to such a harshness of tone from her, he felt the shock of her words to his heart. "I—I can't work the second problem, miss…"

"Indeed?" She pushed back her chair with a movement of her foot. "Indeed! You cannot solve it. After all the explanations I gave you? Then, were you not listening to me?"

He remained silent, his head lowered.

"You see, you did not listen to me," she said quietly. "If you had done so, you would have been able to solve this problem." She repeated her former explanation, and handed him back his exercise book. "Now write out the solution. And be quick!"

In three minutes it was done. Harriet nodded her approval; then she rose.

"Come," she said. "You have given clear proof of your intention, and that must not happen again. I shall have to punish you."

A weakness seized him. He felt his knees giving way. He tried to speak, but could not. He was conscious of his governess' face above him, suddenly seeming darker, and that her eyes were shining.

She stepped back from him and picked up the light ruler. "No, Richard," she said sharply. "Stand where you are. I am going to punish you by giving you ten good strokes on each hand. Do you understand?"

He was staring at her face in terror, unable to utter a word.

"Answer me! Do you understand?"

He gave a moan of acquiescence.

"Very good. Now, hold out your right hand. No, farther out. And higher than that. Higher, I said! Yes, that will do." With her own left hand she reached out and straightened his fingers. Then she raised the ruler slowly and held it poised in the air, at the same time studying his face with a kind of sensual speculation.

His eyes were fixed in terrified fascination on the ruler. Deliberately she held her hand for a few seconds longer, savouring to the full his fear and suspense, then suddenly brought it down with all the force of her wrist.

The boy gave a gasp of agony. The next instant he was shaking his hand as of to work it loose from the arm itself.

Harriet smiled. "Now, the other hand, please."

He looked at her as if unable to believe what was happening to him. With a fearful effort he found his tongue. "Miss—oh please. I can't bear it!"

Her smile vanished. "Nonsense, Richard. Come now, hold out your other hand. At once!"

Trembling violently, he slowly extended his hand, closing his eyes. This time the lash of the ruler drew a sharp cry from him.

"Now the right hand again," said Harriet calmly. "Come, do not keep me waiting."

He obeyed blindly. But when the third stroke had fallen he gave a sharp scream and fell on his knees. The pain was such as he had never believed possible. The eyes he turned on his tormentress were like those of a hunted animal.

Harriet's slender brows drew together. "Get up at once, Richard," she said sharply. "You are behaving very badly. Get up at once, I said, and take the rest of your punishment properly."

"Oh, no—no!" he cried. "I—I can't, miss! I can't!" And suddenly he scrambled to his feet and began stumbling blindly towards the door.

Harriet's face became terrible. She stepped forward, caught him by the arm and pulled him towards her. "Did you hear me?" she said, in a low voice that cut through his pain and his panic. "Your hand sir! And do not try to escape again, or you will regret it."

All at once, penetrated by a nameless terror that dwarfed even his physical suffering, he managed to hold out his hand again. After that, he could remember nothing but the nightmare of the regularly descending ruler and the impression of his palms being mercilessly beaten into a kind of fiery numbness. By the time the torture was over he was screaming steadily, holding his hands before him like a dog, stamping his feet in the total abandonment of his agony.

Harriet drew a deep breath, steadying herself with a powerful effort to resume her calm. She laid the ruler down and gazed at him with a tight smile.

"I hope," she said, "that will cure your inattention in class. And this will be a warning to you of how I intend to punish you in the future. It is firm handling that you need, I see, and you shall have it. Do you understand?"

"Yes, miss," he whispered.

"Then dry your eyes and come here."

He obeyed, suddenly finding himself almost unable to walk. He was as if stupefied. An intense heat was devouring his beaten flesh, seeming to penetrate from his smarting palms to his very shoulders. He felt an overpowering disturbance of his nerves; but the impression of shame and sensuality dominated every sensation.

Harriet continued looking at him with a faintly mocking glance. "You are now forgiven," she said. "And you will try to pay more attention in future, will you not?"

"Yes, miss."

"Then come here and kiss me. That is the way all your punishments will end, with a kiss."

It was she, however, who kissed him. Taking his head between her hands, the one cool and soft, the other still burning from its prolonged grasp of the ruler, she pressed her lips to Richard's. She closed her eyes, so sweet was the melting sensation she received in her loins, from this contact with the boy whom she had just beaten so savagely.

"And now go upstairs and wash," she said. "Tea will be ready in fifteen minutes."

He reached the bathroom in a daze, conscious only of a need so overpowering that it swept away all his resolution of the past week. With numb and shaking hands, he shot the bolt of the door. In a moment he had managed to fumble open his trousers and free his wildly erected member. With a few agonized strokes of his tortured fingers, he released the hoarded sperm of his loins in an ejaculation so violent that he reeled and almost fell in the excess of his sensations. Then, falling weakly into a chair, he put his burning hands to his face and burst into a storm of tears.

The first punishment, and its sequel of an almost compulsive self-indulgence, had a profound effect on the boy. The two were now ever associated. He recalled constantly his governess' words, her tone of cold wrath. He saw again those eyes glowering with the light of determination, those stately gestures, the merciless line of her mouth. He could still feel in imagination the burning smart of the ruler wielded by her strong hand.

But he experienced a strange fascination in remembering these things. The boundless tenderness he had secretly felt for the young woman was being translated into a desire, ardent but still imprecise, to be once again scolded, even punished—to tremble before her, to feel her imperious and powerful while he himself was all weakness and submission.

So he relived in thought those moments of intense emotion when he had been humbled and beaten. He loved his governess only the more for them, but he loved her more secretly. Now, he found a limitless pleasure simply in brushing against her lightly, in touching her as if by chance, and most of all in receiving every evening the kiss she bestowed on him in bed. And every night, alone in the dark, he recounted his pain and reenacted his pleasure in a prolonged orgy of self-gratification.

The qualms of remorse which so often trouble the adolescent on the score of such indulgence had always been quite foreign to him. His sole concern had simply been to conceal the practice from those who might interrupt or prevent his pleasure. This had presented little difficulty before Harriet's arrival. Now, however, his ingenuity was severely taxed. Harriet's supervision of him was close and unremitting. She was with him from morning to night, and the occasions of his privacy were now, in effect, confined to the short periods allotted to natural functions. In spite of this he had been able to procure orgasm several times a day. Any arrears of pleasure were invariably paid off in full at night.

But for all his precautions he sensed that Harriet was well aware of his indulgence. Nothing, he was sure, could escape the survey of those fine grey eyes. What then was restraining her from action? He had no idea. And so, in striving to account for her apparent laxity, he was reduced to supposing that she was biding her time until she had indisputable evidence of his guilt, that she was in fact simply waiting to catch him in the act.

But Harriet, well understanding that the immediate cause of her pupil's sensuality was the presence and image of herself, was quite satisfied with a turn of affairs that indeed fitted only too well into her plans.

One afternoon when she had gone out late she showed him, on her return, a long narrow parcel. "This is for you," she said; and without further explanation she told him to take it to her room.

That evening after dinner she opened the parcel and displayed a slender waxed cane.

He drew in his breath sharply. She watched him as his gaze moved rapidly from the instrument to her face and back again.

"You remember," she said quietly, "what I said would happen if I caught you at that disgraceful habit of yours. I am beginning to think my words had no effect." She paused, and her voice suddenly became cutting. "Be very careful, Richard. You do not know what it is to be really punished—no, not yet. So far you have only had the ruler on your hands, like a child. The strap and the cane are proper instruments for a boy your age, and they are applied in a different and more sensitive place altogether. I warn you they are extremely painful. It rests entirely with you whether I shall have to use them or not. Do you understand me?"

While she was speaking his color had turned from red to pale. He could not take his eyes from this mysterious implement of punishment before him.

"Yes, miss," he murmured.

"Very well. We will say prayers now, and then you will go to bed. But I advise you to consider your actions very carefully when you are in bed tonight."

She listened, as usual, with bent head while he recited the evening prayers, but her mind was busy elsewhere. The question that was beating insistently in her eager brain had long since become reduced to the simple proportions assumed by hunger in all its forms...how long, how long?

CHAPTER SIX

I t was only the following afternoon when Bridget tapped at the schoolroom door.

"What is it, Bridget?" Harriet's eyes had begun to glitter

The old woman beckoned and Harriet went to the door, where they conferred for a few moments. A piece of paper changed hands. The governess came back.

"Come in, Bridget," she said, "and close the door." She turned to Richard; her expression ominous. "Something has arisen that calls for an explanation. Perhaps you have already guessed what it is?"

His expression was black. "N—no, miss..."

She looked at him closely. "Then I will begin by asking you a question. Have you been playing with yourself lately? Come now, speak up."

He had grown as red as fire. He did not know what may come. He gave an agonized glance towards Bridget, then in mute appeal to Harriet.

"Have you? Speak up, I said."

"No, miss. Oh, no."

"No? You are quite sure," she consulted the old woman again.

"Yes," he lied.

"Bridget, you hear what Master Richard says?"

"Indeed I do, ma'am," said the old woman. Her tone was one of outrage, but did not hide a hint of mockery and malice.

Harriet spread her billowing skirts and sat down. "Come here, Richard. Stand in front of me. So. Now, you have already said you have not indulged in that filthy habit of yours lately. Bridget and I have both heard you deny it. Before we go any further, I wish you to know there is only one fault I abominate as deeply as immorality, and that is lying. And I am accustomed to punishing both with equal severity, Therefore, Richard, if you are guilty of the one, do not risk doubling your punishment by persisting in the other. Is that clear?"

The boy's face had become livid. Only too conscious of his guilt, only too well aware that his governess had known of it for some time, he now found himself in a position where to admit his indulgence was impossible—above all in the presence of the servant. The real question was: What did she know? And if she did know, how had she found out? He was silent.

Harriet looked at him calmly; but at her side her hand clenched itself triumphantly.

"Very well, sir. You persist in your denial. And in that case, will you kindly explain how this came to be in the toilet?"

With these words, she held out the crumpled paper in her hand, in which the evidence of an ejaculation was clotted in a small gluey pool. The pallor of the boy's cheeks became leaden. He was still unable to speak.

Harriet remained motionless, her hand out-stretched. When she spoke again her tone was dry. "You have no explanation then? You cannot tell us how this disgusting proof of sensuality came to be where Bridget found it this morning? Come now, my boy, you must know something about this. Answer me."

He tried to reply, but his emotion was so great that he was seized with a violent fit of coughing which left him as red as he had been pale an instant before.

Harriet waited patiently until his coughing ceased, and then repeated her question. "I am waiting for your answer," she added quietly.

"M-m-miss," he stammered, "I—I don't know how it happened."

Harriet's gaze became terrible. "Indeed? You do not know! That is strange. That is altogether strange." Her lip curled scornfully. "See now, there are only the two of us who use that room, Richard. I hope, for your sake, that you are not implying this stuff has any connection with me. Answer! Is that what you mean?"

Richard, distracted with shame and confusion, wrung his hands while the tears poured down his cheeks. "Please, miss," he managed to say at last, "I—I tried not to. Really, I did—"

"Then you disobeyed me last night, even after my clear warning?"

"Oh, I—I couldn't help it…"

"Exactly. You couldn't help it. In other words, you wantonly abused yourself last night, even after I had warned you about what would happen if you did. And now, to crown your horrible sensuality, you have just tried to lie your way out of it. Very well, Bridget, you may go. Master Richard will be whipped."

The old woman remained where she was. The malicious look she had worn throughout the scene gave way to open-mouthed astonishment. "Whipped?"

"Certainly. Do you consider, by any chance, that he has not deserved it?"

"Oh, no ma'am. I—I certainly," said Bridget. "But I didn't think, at Master Richard's age—well, that ..."

Harriet smiled slightly. "His age makes no difference. I shall whip him this evening after dinner. I am telling you now, Bridget, so that you need not be alarmed when you hear us upstairs tonight. You may go."

When Bridget had gone the lesson was resumed as if nothing had happened. But now Richard, covered with shame, hardly dared raise his eyes to his instructress. Harriet, however, remained as clam as she had been before the old woman's appearance, speaking to her pupil with all her customary evenness of tone, attending as usual to the smallest points of detail that arose in the course of their work.

The study period came to an end and she dismissed him with a pleasant smile. The dinner hour arrived, and she took her place as usual opposite him at table. Neither during this time, nor at dinner, did she make any further allusion to the correction awaiting him. But when he had folded his napkin, risen and spoken the short prayer that followed every meal, Harriet also rose, opened a drawer and drew out the cane, which she presented to him silently. His features suddenly became terribly discomposed.

"Take the cane to your room, Richard," she said. "Leave it on your bedside table and go to bed at once without saying your prayers. You will say them with me as usual, after I have whipped you. Go!"

Whimpering slightly, he took the instrument of his approaching torment from her and left the room. On his way to his room he gripped it in a sudden access of childish rage, thinking for a moment he would like to break it across his knee, to throw it out of the window or into the fire. But the next moment he was seized by a sickly, shrinking curiosity that made him examine it carefully.

The cane was of the finest and almost flexible rattan, thinner than those used in English schools and reformatories, and also slightly longer. The greater length, Harriet had found, gave this instrument an increased elasticity that enabled her to inflict maximum pain with least effort.

Richard struck his palm lightly with it, wincing at the cruelty of its bite. Then, throwing it on the table in the middle of the room, he dropped face downwards on his bed with a groan of mingled fury and despair. But almost immediately he leapt up again in fear, lest Miss Marwood surprise him in this posture.

Not for an instant did he entertain the idea of resisting his governess. Not only was such an idea foreign to his soft and passive disposition, but the strange sensual weakness which swept over him at the sight and even thought of this woman's anger would have prevented him from putting it into practice. And so, breathless, his flesh twitching nervously, with a prickling sensation of the skin and a tingling in his fingers and toes, he found himself unable to do anything but wait, in terror mingled with anticipation, for the arrival of the young tyrant.

The period of waiting lasted a long time.

Several times, he heard the sound of her footsteps approaching his door, and his emotion mounted to a pitch of intensity. But each time the steps receded and died away, bringing him a momentary relief that was soon swallowed up by his returning trepidation. The hours went slowly by.

Harriet Marwood, as we may already suspect, was mistress of all refinements of punishment. She was quite conscious of her pupil's state of mind, and in thus prolonging his suspense she not only made sure of reducing him to absolute docility but also ministered to her own taste for the infliction of a subtle and delicate species of torment.

From each visit she paid to the boy's door, in the intervals of her leisurely progress of undressing, she returned to her own room with a heightened color and a brighter eye. Looking in her mirror, she could admire the face whose diabolical beauty was sensibly increased by her imagination of the effect produced on the boy by each of these tantalizing trips. When she was at last ready for the business before her she parted the long cape she wore and examined the image of her own magnificent nudity in the glass with a sensual and speculative eye. Her hands lifted and caressed the points of her breasts, then passed down slowly and luxuriously over her belly...

It was ten o'clock before Richard saw the door of his room open. At that instant he felt nothing but a boundless surge of relief for the ending of his suspense, which was immediately followed by a paralyzing shock of fear as he saw his governess herself.

She was clad in a long, dark dressing cape whose straight severe folds, falling unbroken from her shoulders to the floor concealed altogether the outlines of her figure, giving her a stark conventual air. It was in no way dispelled by the effect of her beautiful arms, bare to the shoulder, emerging from two long openings on either side, a display in which there was a suggestion of intimacy and the assurance of the greatest freedom of movement. A small hood, hanging loosely on her back, added a further touch of the bizarre.

This cape, we must remark in passing, obviously meant much to Harriet, though its actual associations we have as yet no means of knowing. But her choice of it on this occasion would suggest that she had worn it many times before and in situations similar to the present—that it was in fact the costume appropriated by her for all ceremonial and exceptional severities. This is the only explanation we can furnish for her voluptuous gestures a few minutes before—as if there were concealed in its long heavy folds, like some exquisite and troubling perfume, the fancied echo of screams, the whistle of cane and whip, and the sight of helpless and writhing flesh.

Richard was gazing at her, sick with terror as he grasped the significance for himself of this costume. The next moment he was seized by a violent shudder, as the appearance of this figure in his room irresistibly recalled that of the medieval torturer, smocked, hooded, bare-armed, whip in hand, pictured in an old illustrated book in the library: from Miss Marwood's pale hand hung a thin, curling brown leather strap.

She closed the door behind her, turned the key in the lock, and advanced to the bed beside which he was standing. Her face was pale, her eyes aglitter and her expression one of extraordinary severity.

"Why are you not in bed?" she asked.

He made no reply. He remained standing before her, his arms dangling at his sides, trembling in every limb.

"I told you to be in bed," she said. "Once more you have disobeyed me. It appears I shall have to whip you every day before you learn the habit of obedience. Get undressed at once!"

He turned on her an imploring look, clasping his hand as he stammered, "Miss, I—I'm sorry for what I did. If you please, forgive me—"

She shook her head. "No, Richard. I will not tolerate sensuality and lying! Hurry and do as ordered."

With a moan of despair he began to take off his clothes. When only his shirt remained, Harriet reached out to take his hand and draw him towards her. He avoided her grasp and took a step backwards.

Harriet's nose wrinkled with sudden rage. She controlled herself with an effort: "Ah, this is too much," she said, throwing the strap on the chair. "After all that has happened, you still dare resist me. You shall smart for this, sir."

With a swift movement she raised her hands and drew the close-fitting hood over her head, confining her long, heavy hair. Thus prepared, she stepped forward.

The effect of the gesture made the boy turn pale. He shrank from this hooded figure, now even

more terrifying, crying out, "Miss, please! I'm
sorry—I won't move..." But still, as she came
towards him, he backed against the wall beside
his bed in terror.

Harriet raised her bare arm and slapped his
cheek with such force that he reeled and fell sideways over his bed.

He staggered to his feet, his fists at his temples,
half stunned. She pulled one of his arms down
and another slap, still harder than the first, threw
him back on the bed.

"So, you will resist me!" she repeated.

He slipped off the bed to his knees, shivering,
turning on her a look of terror-stricken incredulity.

"Now will you obey me?" She was almost out
of breath, as much from her exertions as from the
heady sensation she experienced from an act of
purely physical domination.

He stared at her in silence, like a beaten animal.

"Get up!"

He rose slowly to his feet, his arms raised
defensively before him.

"Put your hands down! And look at me."

He obeyed. She drew a deep breath and bent
her gaze on her pupil's wide eyes, terrified and
filled with tears. They remained looking at each
other silently for a few instants. Then a strange
smile parted the governess' lips. "Now kiss me,"
she said. "And promise me you will submit in the
future."

Looking at the beautiful grey eyes now suddenly grown soft and swimming, the boy emitted
a deep sob, a moan of pleasure. A veritable ecstasy flooded him as he abandoned himself entirely

to the woman's will. He put his arms around her neck and pressed his trembling lips to the severe mouth.

"Oh, miss, I promise..." he murmured.

"Very good," she said, pushing him away. "Now we will continue. You know why I am here, Richard, and that I mean to whip you without mercy. We have delayed too long already. On to the bed with you now—face down, please."

With the calm of despair, he obeyed, the muscles of his buttocks already contracting spasmodically under his shirt at the prospect of the pain to come.

But Harriet was not yet ready to begin. From the inner pocket of her cape she produced four bracelets of thick braided leather, each terminating in a strap and buckle. "Give me your hands," she said.

"Miss!" he cried, struck with panic at the idea of being fastened to his bed. "Oh, please—no! I promise you, I'll—I'll lie still!"

"No, Richard." She slipped the bracelets over his unresisting wrists, drew them tight, and buckled the straps to the posts of the heavy iron bed. Then she fastened his ankles in the same way, drawing the straps taut so that the boy's body was straight and secure. When this was done she raised his shirt and pulled it over his head.

This was the moment for which she had waited ever since she saw him almost three weeks ago. The boy's swelling buttocks were now displayed before her, naked, beautiful, and at her mercy, as she had always desired them. She paused for a few delicious moments, savouring her anticipations, feasting with sombre satisfaction on the sight of this virgin expanse of puerile flesh now at last ready for her to whip as long and severely as she wished. Then, with a deep voluptuous sigh, she picked up the leather strap...

❖ ❖ ❖

Downstairs in the dining room, through which she was passing, Bridget heard the muffled cries from overhead. She stopped in surprise, then remembering, she nodded her head and remained listening eagerly.

The cries continued, mounting steadily in shrillness and frequency, accompanied by the slow, regular sounds of the descending strap. A minute went by, then another, and another, and still the rhythm of the blows and cries continued inexorably. The old woman's expression changed gradually from smiling approval to admiration, to amazed incredulity, at last to simple awe. "Lord," she muttered at last, "that young woman don't believe in doing things by halves!"

The sounds died away and were succeeded by faint groans. The old woman remained standing in the darkness of the dining room, listening intently. Soon the cries recommenced, now more agonized than ever...

In the room upstairs, Richard was being subjected to punishment of a rigor he had never dreamed of.

Here, indeed, we may say that the extent of an English governess' severity sixty years ago is almost inconceivable to those brought up in the softer educational climates of Europe or America. Only the upper-class English child of that period knew what it was to be flogged in slow and leisurely stages to the utmost limits by a firm and experienced woman, further than would be believed possible. Richard Lovel was now receiving his first taste of these English methods, which would be applied to him with stern and loving care in the years to come.

Harriet had just finished strapping him. He was still moaning weakly from the ordeal. His thighs as well as his buttocks, all the flesh from his knees to his waist, were now a sheet of uniform glowing scarlet, testifying to the merciless skill with which the instrument had been applied. She looked at her work impassively for a few moments, then uncovered the boy's head, noting with satisfaction that the muscles of his face and neck were still working convulsively.

Richard's great dark blue eyes, wide with fear, were lifted to hers. He tried to speak, but was prevented by the sobs that kept rising to his throat.

Harriet looked at him with a faint smile, drawing the strap caressingly through her fingers. "That was not pleasant, was it, Richard? I think if you had known of the effects of this strap of mine you would have thought twice before giving in to that habit of self-abuse again, I daresay you are also getting to know me a little better, and how I deal with boys like you. At any rate, I promise you that before I am through with you tonight you will know what a good whipping is."

His eyes filled with horror. "Then—then, miss—it's not finished?"

Harriet's thoughtful smile deepened. "No, Richard. I am afraid your poor buttocks must suffer still more punishment this evening." She laid down the strap, and picking up the cane, she made it whistle through the air several times, studying her pupil's frightened face and wildly shaking loins with a dreamy, rapt expression.

"You have still to taste this new cane, you know."

"But, miss—please! Please—I—I can't stand any more..."

Her only answer was to cut him sharply across the thighs. As he screamed, she studied his face intently, her eyes glowing softly.

"Ah," she said gently, "you will just have to stand it, I am afraid. Keep telling yourself that you are being whipped for your own good." Deliberately, she drew the shirt over his head again. "That may help you to bear the pain more manfully..."

Then, pressing a hand to her breast which had begun to palpitate deliciously, she began lashing the boy's swollen loins with short, vigorous strokes of her powerful wrist. The sharper pain caused by the cane, in contrast with that of the strap, was at once manifested by shrill screams and an almost epileptic writhing of the buttocks as they sought to escape the bite of this famous instrument of scholastic discipline...

❖ ❖ ❖

"Hark now, Arthur!"

Mr. Lovel, dozing beside his mistress in his own wing of the great house, returned to consciousness at the sound of her low vibrant voice. He raised himself in bed and listened for a few moments to the sounds coming to him faintly.

"Good heavens," he said, laughing. "Is that Richard? Our Miss Marwood is certainly taking her duties to heart, isn't she?"

"She surely is," replied his mistress. "Only listen to the boy! You'd think he was being murdered. Ah well, it's all for his own good, isn't it?"

"Hm-mmm, yes," he said, and then paused, cocking his head as another scream of particular intensity bored up through the thick walls and flooring, "What can she be beating him with, do you think, to make him howl like that?"

"Oh, that will be a cane or horsewhip, Arthur. It is what they use on a grown boy, you know."

"A horsewhip! By Jove, you women are cold-blooded creatures at times, Kate."

She laughed. "No, it's only that we cannot bear a habit that's like to stint us of our due." Her hand automatically strayed to her protector's genitals. To her surprise she found his own hand ahead of her. "Saints defend us, Arthur—what are you at there? Why, you'll be needing the whip yourself at this rate! Ah, leave off that stroking of yourself, my dear. It's a woman's office to do that for her man…"

Arthur surrendered his member to her hands and lay back in the bed again, a prey to disturbing but delicious impressions, listening to the sharp cries from the room beneath while Kate's fingers teased and tickled and massaged his slowly stiffening member.

"Oh," she said after a few moments, "that is bringing you up now, isn't it? Or is that all that's doing it, tell me?"

"By God, Kate," he murmured softly, "I hardly know…"

Kate laughed indulgently. "Well, give yourself no trouble if it is. I've known many a man to get an erection when there's any kind of whipping going forward. God knows why, but it's fact. And in that case I had best suck you out now, for you'll be wanting to spend before that Miss Marwood is finished flogging the poor boy. It cannot be long, I'm thinking, for surely the poor child cannot stand much more. Come, let me suck you now, and you just lie back and listen."

"No, Kate." Arthur sat up suddenly, and his hands sought her thighs. "By God, I want you as a woman tonight. Get on your back, and let me into your womb…"

"God in heaven above," Kate cried, laughing as she obeyed, "what's this that has taken you, that you are reforming your ways altogether! You've not taken me like this for more years than I can remember, Arthur. Oh, but it's good, it's wonderfully good for a change, isn't it?"

Mr. Lovel made no reply but to drive his member deeply into her. As the screams far below continued steadily in an agonized crescendo he kept thrusting with a stroke as insistent and regular as the blows that were falling on the writhing young body in the room beneath.

❖ ❖ ❖

Harriet, too, was being carried to the heights of pleasure. The clear whistling of the cane, the shrieking of the boy, and the sight of the helpless flesh now crossed with the long welts she had raised with the skillful lash of the cane, afforded her at last the special, savage enjoyment her peculiar nature craved.

She had become rather pale. Short, languorous sighs escaped her with every stroke. The bridge of her nose was furrowed with a small wrinkle, her nostrils quivered, flaring widely as if she were breathing some intoxicating perfume, and her tight-lipped mouth was twitching with emotion. She struck hard, her arm descending evenly, methodically, with a superb mastery of aim and effort. Had it rested with her own appetite alone, she would have continued the punishment indefinitely. But her self-possession, which in the midst of her wildest excesses never deserted her, made her cease at last. By then, indeed, it was time for the chastisement to stop. Richard, at the end of his strength, had ceased to cry out at all.

She unfastened him, ordered him to remain as he was, and then, wetting a towel in the basin, laid it gently on the burning flesh. After a few minutes she took the boy in her arms and sitting on the bed, made him stand before her. He was sobbing with exhaustion, barely able to remain on his feet.

Harriet looked at his distress with entire satisfaction. This was how she liked to see a boy! She smiled into his still distorted face.

"I hope that will help cure you of that practice of playing with your genitals, Richard. Do you think it will?"

"Y-yes, miss," he groaned weakly.

"Come, come! You are making too much of an old-fashioned whipping, my boy. No more of this nonsensical whining, please! Kneel down in front of me."

He sank to his knees, his hands imprisoned in hers.

"Now say, 'Thank you, miss, for having corrected me. I ask your pardon for the trouble you have taken, and I promise to try not to abuse myself any more.'"

He repeated the humiliating words with docility.

"Very good," she said, the ghost of a smile curving her full lips. "And now—prayers!"

In a voice at first choked with sobs, but which towards the end became firmer and more controlled, he recited the evening prayer as he stood before her in his shirt.

"Now take off your shirt and go to bed."

As he did so she gave an exclamation, and the

flush her cheeks had worn since the beginning of the punishment became deeper. The boy's penis had already begun to swell. He turned on her an agonized look; but she appeared to pay no further attention to this circumstance. He got into bed swiftly.

She drew the covers over him gently, then bent over and kissed him, softly and voluptuously, on the mouth. He did not close his eyes, but kept his gaze fixed in ecstasy on the beautiful flushed face, framed in its shirred hood, which was brought so close to his own

"You are forgiven," she said, smiling at him. "But I advise you, Richard, to behave yourself in future. You will try, won't you?"

He said nothing, staring at her in fascination.

"Good night, Richard."

"Good night, miss."

And the governess regained her room, where she sank into an armchair facing the mirror which gave back a reflection of her caped and hooded figure. Luxuriously she opened her cape and parted her thighs. Her mouth was now soft and humid, her eyes glistening...

Upstairs, Arthur Lovel was still panting in the utter exhaustion induced by the most violent and pleasurable orgasm he had ever known. In the darkness of his room, his son was already rubbing his wildly erected member in a veritable ecstasy of pain, humiliation, and rapture.

PART TWO
CHAPTER ONE

With the month of June, the full heat of summer descended on London. The dusty streets, now almost empty, baked in the glare of sunlight, and the air was parched and quivering. On Great Portland Street the few trees supplied only the scantiest shade.

The interior of Arthur Lovel's sombre house had become metamorphosed by the clear, searching light that penetrated into corners and recesses. The shadows of winter, which had seemed so native to these large dark rooms, were dispelled. The house, indeed, seemed to have a rather uncomfortable air, as if light and sunshine had really no business in it. Even the schoolroom had taken on a new aspect: the furniture of walnut and old oak had lost its grim and surly character, and a certain black leather armchair, on which Richard was now obliged to kneel, his buttocks bared to receive the cane or ruler, had almost an air of dullness and respectability.

The boy had just had his birthday. During the winter, he had grown taller and heavier; but it was noticeable that the effeminacy of his appearance had increased also. Moreover, if his figure was still slim, his thighs and loins had taken on further breadth, an amplitude that was emphasized by the close fit of the Eton jacket and trousers he still wore. On the other hand, his member, whose erections were now still more apparent beneath the tightly stretched serge of the latter, had retained all its puerile proportions and almost childish grace.

Since Harriet Marwood had definitely adopted the method of corporal punishment to bring him to her idea of perfection—the end to which she was passionately devoted—scarcely a day had gone by without her having had recourse to the whip. His education in the article of discipline had indeed progressed remarkably. By now, like any other English boy under the authority of a governess, he had learned to resign all judgment to his instructress. He had acquired the habit of instant obedience and he had learned to submit to the most vigorous flogging without question.

Nor was this all. At least one evening every fortnight, strapped to his bed, he endured the protracted torment of a double correction with strap and cane. These important occasions were no longer announced to him beforehand by the sagacious young woman. Thus, for three or four nights a week, the boy could not be sure whether her nightly visit portended the rapture of an evening kiss or the ordeal of a special punishment—an uncertainty resolved only at the last moment by her appearing either fully clothed and

with an affectionate smile on her lips, or in her
long hooded cape, bare-armed and with the terrible strap in her hand. Therefore his anticipations
and even his emotions of pleasure and pain were
confounded in a single framework of exquisite tension.

By such treatment he had been brought to an
extraordinary height of sensitivity—and also of
sensuality. Living in a state of constant nervous
trepidation, at the mercy of all the whims of his
instructress, he had come to entertain a highly
ambiguous attitude toward her. He feared her and
he loved her—but his love was as yet almost
entirely sensual. Her hold on him was through the
flesh, but it was maintained and increased by the
bestowal of the exact contrary of caresses. The latter he dispensed to himself; with her stern and
charming image before his mind. He was happy in
the vicarious enjoyment of her which he obtained
in this way.

As for Harriet herself, her temperament
seemed to find full satisfaction in the imposition of
such a regime. Why or how we do not know. To
bring a beaten and degraded look into a boy's face,
to rend self-respect out of him in fear, is an occupation not especially relished by the ordinary
woman. Nor is the deliberate process of associat-
ing punishment and pleasure in such a boy's mind.
But Harriet Marwood was not an ordinary woman.
Her sensuality was of an antique kind that found
its proper element in a curious combination of
maternal protectiveness and cold-blooded cruelty.
Now, infatuated with her pupil's face and figure,
she was happy in her absolute mastery of him.

But perhaps happier than either governess or
pupil were Arthur Lovel and his mistress. For him,

with Kate available at every hour of the day or
night, life had become an almost ceaseless round
of sensual indulgence. His reawakened interest in
the charms of her vulva now constituted only an
added variety of enjoyment. Thus with his ejaculations shared between her womb, her rectum, and
her mouth, fornication, sodomizing and being
sucked, and for variety his enjoyment of the cunning manipulations of her hands, feet and breasts,
the worthy man of business exploited to the full his
gargantuan capacity for orgasm. He literally wal-
lowed in his own and his mistress' sperm.

Indeed, he could never have enough of Kate,
nor she of him. Even their occasional fits of utter
exhaustion were at once dispelled by the invigorat-
ing sounds of flagellation that reached them every
day from the schoolroom and every night from
Richard's and Harriet's sleeping quarters. The
house on Great Portland Street had become in fact
an abode of unbridled sensuality, no less intense
from its very discreetness and formality, or by its
characteristically English qualities of method and
reserve.

Harriet, well aware of this, was nonetheless concerned with its possible effect on her own plans.
She was especially troubled lest Richard's own
sensuality be diverted from herself and corrupted
by the example of a more equal sexual relationship
exemplified by Kate and his father. I must get the
boy away from all this, she thought: I must have
him to myself.

Her opportunity came one afternoon when Mr.
Lovel inquired as to the progress of his son's cure.

"Why, sir," she said thoughtfully, "I have been
able to hold him in check. But the habit of self-
gratification is very deeply rooted, and calls for the

most severe measures. I have been obliged to thrash him almost constantly."

"Yes, yes, indeed," said Mr. Lovel, his eye gleaming for an instant, "and I've no doubt it's doing him a world of good. You must not spare him, Miss Marwood."

"No, sir, I shall not. And I shall cure him, you may rest assured. You can see for yourself the improvement in his appearance." She paused, and a slight frown came to her forehead as she went on. "But it is now Midsummer, sir. Living in town, in this heat, is not good for a boy of Richard's age and delicate constitution. We ought really to go to the country for a month or two. Did you not tell me, sir, that you had a property somewhere in the country?"

"In Hampshire? Of course!" exclaimed Mr. Lovel. "In fact, why don't you go down to Christchurch with Richard? That will do him a world of good! Exactly, Christchurch. An excellent idea."

Harriet cloaked a smile of triumph. When she broke the news to Richard, he too seemed deeply moved.

"We will go to Christchurch together," she said. "Down there I shall have you under my authority even more completely than here. I will make you a well behaved boy indeed, Richard!" She looked at him affectionately. "Well, are you glad to be going to the country with me? To live there with me, just the two of us alone?"

"Yes! Oh yes, miss…"

She took him in her arms and kissed him with such warmth that his head reeled. And for her part, as she clasped his yielding loins to her and felt the timid pressure of his member against her thighs, she was deliciously aware of her own genitals being bathed in the voluptuous moisture of anticipation.

CHAPTER TWO

Mr. Lovel's house in Christchurch was situated a little beyond the outskirts of the town, in the middle of the country and not far from the Stout, the pretty river that flows into the Avon a short distance farther on. At her first glimpse of it, Harriet was enchanted. She noted its utter seclusion, the heavily wooded grounds, and the high brick wall that encircled the entire property. What a place to bring a boy, she thought, her breast swelling with exultation.

As soon as they arrived, she summoned Molly, the caretaker's wife, and gave her instructions in her duties. The governess had already planned their life in detail. Molly was to do the housework in the early morning and prepare the breakfast, and neither she nor her husband were to set foot in the house at any other time of the day. The old couple occupied the small lodge at the entrance to the grounds, and thus had no further business in the house itself. A caterer in the town would simply plan the menu and leave instructions. In this way she and Richard would be always alone and undisturbed.

"And," she said to herself, "this is where I shall really break him in. Oh, the fine floggings I can give him here! How I shall make him suffer and scream now that there is no one to overhear! And how thoroughly I shall corrupt him, how deeply I will make him love me before I am through!"

His room adjoined hers and Harriet took care that the door between them should remain open all night.

One evening a few days after their arrival she said to him, "I hear you stirring in your bed a good deal, Richard. You toss and turn and fidget. Are you sure you are behaving yourself?"

As always, the question filled him with shame and confusion. "Oh yes, miss," he lied.

Harriet smiled to herself. "But you are a long time getting to sleep, are you not?"

He mumbled an inaudible reply.

"This evening you will come and read to me in bed. That will leave you tired and able to fall asleep sooner."

That night, after they had said prayers in her room, she put a novel of Mrs. Edgeworth's into his hands. "I am going to bed now. You will remain here while I get ready, and then you will read to me."

"Yes, miss." He was obviously carried to the height of excitement by the prospect.

Harriet looked at him impassively, savouring the pleasure she took in his nervous disturbance. "Leave your book on the table for the present,

while you help me undress. Come here and unlace
my shoes." She sat down on the edge of the bed,
drew up her skirt and crossed her legs. Richard
watched her in a virtual stupor.

"Well," she said. "What are you waiting for?
Down on your knees, sir, and undo my shoes."

He knelt and began to unfasten the laces from
the highly arched foot, which, encased in its high-
heeled shoe of supple fawn leather, was swinging
under his nose. He noted the slenderness of her
ankle. He saw her leg also in its fine transparent
silk stocking, the hem of a white petticoat, and the
lace of her drawers. His hands trembled as he
untied the shoelaces. When he drew off the shoe
itself his excitement was such that he let it fall on
her other foot.

"Idiot!" said Harriet. She leaned forward and
slapped his face swiftly. "Pay attention how you
take off the other, if you please."

The warm, intimate odor of her unshod feet put
his senses in a fever. He rose from his knees, trembling slightly.

"You would make a poor lady's maid," smiled
Harriet, standing up. "Go and sit down now, and
wait till I am in bed."

Calmly she began to undress, letting fall first
her skirt, then her petticoat. She removed the
bodice, and then, standing in corset and drawers,
let down her beautiful hair, shaking it out to its
full length so that it fell in a thick wavy mass covering her buttocks, whose firm divided outline
appeared through the fine linen of her drawers.
Then she separated her tresses and swiftly plait-
ed them in two long braids. When this was done,
she removed her corset, drawers and stockings,
and stood in front of Richard in her shift. His

gleaming eyes did not leave her for an instant.

She stepped to the closet from which she took a long silk nightdress, and then deliberately let her shift, which was held only by two straps passing over her beautiful shoulders, fall to the carpet.

She had taken no precautions to shield herself from the boy's gaze. But he, despite the desire he had to see her, had simply not dared keep his eyes on her until the very end. It was only when she turned back towards the bed, clad from neck to heels in the long ribboned gown and holding her shift in her hand, that he realized that for a few moments she had been entirely nude before him. At the thought, his face suddenly glowed a deep red, as if the display, far from having been accomplished by slow gradations, had been made all at once.

She laid the filmy garment, still warm and impregnated with the odor of her magnificent young body, on the back of the armchair where he was sitting, and went into the bathroom.

No sooner had she left him than he turned round, seized the shift and plunged his face into it, breathing in with trembling nostrils the subtle and disturbing perfume that clung in the soft linen creases. Intoxicating himself almost to madness, his penis swelling and stiffening deliciously between his thighs. All at once he heard a step behind him.

Harriet had re-entered the room quietly. As he saw his governess beside him, erect and severe in her long nightdress, her penetrating gaze bent on him, his heart seemed to miss a beat. She saw me! he thought. Mixed with his fear of her anger, however, he was conscious of a peculiar and subtle price.

"Richard, what were you doing?"

He did not reply. She took his head between her hands and forced him to look at her face. "What were you doing?" she repeated. Then she fixed him with a gaze suddenly grown hard and menacing. "Yes," she said, "I saw you! You sensual, wicked boy! Come here."

"Miss..." he mumbled. He was choking with a peculiar excitement. Already he was as if drunk with the sense of his subjection to this female flesh.

Gently, with movements slow and deliberate as those of ritual, she picked up her shift, folded it to make a gag of it, and then bound it over his mouth and nose. The filminess of the material did not hinder his breathing, but every breath was as if taken from between her breasts or thighs. Then she drew him to the bed, and sitting down she clasped him between her knee, opened his trousers and drew out his half-erected member.

With an impression of ecstasy that was boundless, Richard abandoned himself to the touch of her hands. Never before had she done this. Never had he experienced such sensations!

Harriet was indeed a past mistress of the art of titillating a boy's sensitive genitals. It was an art she had acquired through sheer love of doing so, and one she had developed to such a height of refinement that when she wished she could make of it an exercise in cruelty of the most voluptuous kind. And this was her object on the present occasion.

Richard, feeling his penis slowly hardening, breathed deep sighs of pleasure. The delicacy of these fingers was irresistible, their light and leisurely coaxing of the nerves so exquisitely skillful that he was almost fainting with pleasure. Already, used to his own simple and forthright manipulations, he believed he was about to ejaculate. But he found he could not, although the tantalizing insufficiency of these caresses kept him on the verge of relief for several moments.

With an effort he willed his orgasm. The sperm even seemed to collect at the base of his throbbing shaft, and then suddenly he felt the sharp pressure of strong fingers there, cutting off the pleasure, changing it to a sensation of constriction and discomfort. The hands remained locked and motionless.

"No, Richard," he heard her murmuring. "No..."

He remained braced between her knees, trembling with the tantalizing pain in his loins. Then his member slowly relaxed, subsided, and began to soften.

"You see, Richard," she said softly, "you are in my power. You will begin to realize this more and more from now on. You must not think I meant to indulge you in your wickedness. No, what I am doing is only another punishment. With this, and with the whip, I will teach you the habit of self-control. See now..." And her fingers once again resumed their maddening caresses on the drooping bulb and neck of his responsive penis.

Twice more she brought him to the very point of orgasm. The boy, his body jerking and shuddering with the desperation of his desire to let his sperm gush forth, was in a veritable torment of unappeased craving.

But, by now, Harriet had had enough of this cruel and tantalizing game. All at once she released him, and then, taking him in her arms passionately, pressed her lips to his in a long, shuddering kiss.

"Try to behave yourself now!" she said, pushing him away abruptly and slipping between the sheets of her bed. "Hold your book in your left hand, and put your right hand in mine. Just so, my dear. I wish you to have the constant impression of being in my power, of being in my hand..."

He was burning with a fever of the senses, he had no more strength than a two-year-old child. He abandoned his hand to Harriet and began to read.

The reading lasted a long time. In order to turn the pages, he placed the book on the edge of the bed and used his left hand.

Harriet was falling asleep. From time to time Richard darted a swift glance at her, seeing her resting quietly, the two heavy braids of hair framing the noble head, beautiful as that of a goddess. An even breath raised her creamy half-uncovered breast, and he fought down a wild desire to put his lips to the prominent nipple, or at least to imprint a kiss on the soft hand which had caressed his genitals with such cunning and cruelty. Then the great grey eyes half opened and were turned on him.

"Close your book now," she murmured. "Say goodnight to me and go to bed like a good boy. And think of what happened to you this evening, will you not? You will think of it?"

"Yes, miss," he whispered.

He bent over her and respired her warm, perfumed breath as their mouths clung together in the evening kiss.

CHAPTER THREE

But the next day Harriet was colder, more distant, and severer than ever. For trifling reasons, sometimes for none at all, she scolded him, shook him, and slapped his face with such force that he saw stars. Several times during the day, she made him kneel on the floor with his hands beneath his knees while she laid the ruler smartly across his shoulders. Unable to understand the cause of her displeasure, hurt and bewildered, he could do nothing but weep. Had he known that this treatment was simply caused by the irritation of her unappeased desire for him, his anguish might perhaps have been less.

Before dinner she made his tears the pretext for pulling his hair so sharply that he was unable to repress a scream.

"So!" she said, her teeth showing for an instant. "So, you cry out for nothing! I'll give you something to cry about then." She picked up the cane and made it whistle in the air. "Down with your trousers!"

He felt the staggering injustice of the order with such intensity that he retreated a step, flushing hotly.

Harriet drew herself up. "So," she said, her voice suddenly quiet and controlled, "you are not yet cured of your old habit of resistance, are you? I thought as much. No," she said sharply, as he began fumbling in desperate haste with his clothing. "Stay as you are, sir. Go to your room and get into bed at once. You will go without your dinner tonight, and after I have had mine I will pay you a little visit. Not another word. Go!"

Miserably, he went upstairs to his room. Already he was bitterly regretting his impulse of rebellion, as much for the loss of Harriet's favour as for the painful consequences he foresaw. As he undressed slowly and got into bed, he found himself trembling both with fear and remorse. Would it, he asked himself, be one of those terrible evening corrections he had undergone in bed that winter? Surely not, he argued. After all, he had been a good boy and he was on his holidays. His meditations were interrupted by the sudden appearance of Harriet in the doorway.

Without a word she laid a new cane on the table, and then proceeded to draw the heavy curtains against the light of the summer evening.

He followed her movements with surprise and anguished uncertainty. Then, unable to bear the suspense any longer: "Miss," he asked timidly, "please, are—are you going to whip me now?"

Harriet looked at him calmly for a few moments, drinking in the sheer terror of his expression and attitude. "No," she said at last. "I shall come and see you later on, just as I told you."

He shivered, his eyes were raised to her in supplication. "And—and are you going to use the—the strap?" he asked piteously.

Harriet paused, a smile curving her beautiful lips for the first time that day. "I have not yet made up my mind on that point," she said. Then, checking his words of entreaty with a gesture, she said, "Silence, please! You are becoming impertinent, Richard. It will be better for you to employ the next hour considering your misconduct and in resolving to amend it in the future, than wondering about the degree of your punishment." She paused again, picked up the cane and fingered it for a few moments, then laid it down. "I shall consider the whole matter very carefully at dinner," she said. "You will be punished severely, of course. But I assure you it will be no more than you deserve."

His solitary meditations for the next hour and a half were far from pleasant. Tossed between hope and fear, he succeeded in persuading himself—against reason and experience—that he might escape with a sound caning, when he saw the door open to admit his governess.

At his first sight of her he gave a moan of anguish. Harriet was wearing her long cape. In one hand she carried the leather bracelets for his wrist and ankles, and in the other she held the terrible strap.

"Yes," she said quietly. "You are in for it this evening, my boy."

And she was as good as her word.

Now, indeed, she was carried to that seventh heaven none can know or appreciate save the flagellant who has found herself, for the first time, free to carry her severity to the limits of fleshly endurance. Now, she thought, as each blow of her strong and cunning wrist evoked a wild scream of pain, now I can do as I wish with this charming boy! There is no one to hear his cries but me. There is nothing to check or hinder my will.

It was dark outside by the time she finished. By then, Richard had been reduced to a moaning, blubbering mass. His flesh, from the long and vigorous application of strap and cane, was a deep fiery red, latticed with thin dark lines. His cheeks were sodden with tears, the muscles of his throat sore and strained from continual screaming. He lay motionless, conscious of nothing except the enormous relief of knowing that his whipping was over at last.

Harriet laid the cane on the table and sat beside him on the bed.

"You understand now, I hope," she said to him quietly, "how your holidays are to be passed, and that I mean to use them to break you in properly. Here in the country, you see, we are free from interference or interruption, and at last I have the power, as well as the will, to deal with you as you need to be dealt with." She paused and stroked his wet, quivering cheek gently. "You did not think of that, perhaps, when you told me how glad you would be to live alone with me! Now, I trust, you are beginning to know me and my methods a little better. And you will know still more before our holidays are over. I must tell you, Richard, that we shall spend many evenings like this together, you and I…"

He heard her voice, low and sweet, coming to him as if from far away, through the mist of pain, through the agony of his burning flesh, carrying in its tones a healing promise of better things, a guarantee of some unimaginable bliss that shone dimly before him from the horizons of a distant but certain future...

"Yes, yours is a bitter cup, Richard," the beloved voice went on softly. "You may pray, and pray again, in the months and years to come, that it may be put from you. But be sure, if you are sure of anything in the world, that I shall see you drink it to the dregs. For I have but one end in view, my dear, and that is to bring you into the pleasant places prepared for you by your temperament and my love. Take courage, Richard. It will never be more than you can bear. And remember always, if you should doubt or grow fainthearted, that your happiness, the happiness of your whole life, is in the hands of one who loves you more deeply than a mother."

CHAPTER FOUR

The following morning Harriet kissed her pupil affectionately as she wakened him. "Today we are going into Christchurch to do some shopping," she said.

They set out after breakfast. "Give me your hand, Richard," she said when they were in the street. "You are still only a child, and one takes children by the hand. Sometimes," she added with a note of banter, "when you exasperate me too much I tell myself I should put you on a leash, a leather leash, as if you were a little dog."

The passers-by and the gossips standing on corners and in doorways turned a curious gaze on the handsome young woman with the free and imperious bearing, who was leading by the hand the slender timid youth who might have been taken for a girl dressed in boy's clothes.

"Ah, here we are," said Harriet, stopping abruptly at a ropemaker's shop. Telling Richard to wait, she entered. When she emerged she was carrying a small whip of cords at which he cast a look of trepidation. It was, in fact, an English martinet made after the approved model. The handle, made of six strands of whipcord stiffly braided, was short and afforded an excellent grip. The thongs, each tapering to a well-waxed lash whipped with silk, were no more than a foot in length.

Harriet, smiling, made it hiss before the troubled gaze of her pupil, but she said nothing. A few minutes later she drew him into a saddler's shop on the next street, where a dark smiling man came forward, bowing and rubbing his hands ingratiatingly.

"I wish you to make me a leather martinet, of the same size and style as this," said Harriet, laying the whip of cords on the counter.

"Certainly, madam," said the shopman, picking up the instrument of correction with an air of profound respect. "I can have the article made up for you at once, if you wish." He cast a rapid glance at Richard. "You would like it at once?"

"There is no immediate haste. The end of this week will do very well. You will make it of the finest cow-hide, of course. I shall leave this as a model for your workman. I should also like to order a simple harness..."

"Certainly, madam," said the shopman, bowing and rubbing his hands with even greater satisfaction. "We make harnesses of all kinds, for horses, ponies, dogs: single, double, tandem or unicorn hitch—everything, in short. We have the honor of supplying my Lord A—, Sir John B—, Mr. C—, the Member of Parliament, and indeed I may say the entire aristocracy of the county. If you will be so kind as to give me your specifications, madam…"

Harriet cut him short. "I will give them to you now," she said. "For the measurements, you will take them on this young gentleman here."

The shopman, taken aback for an instant, glanced from governess to pupil, and back. Then his face broke into a smile of understanding and appreciation. "A whipping-harness! But of course. I did not understand at first. Quite so, my dear madam. Nothing is simpler, I can have one made up within the week. First, what kind of leather do you wish? We have all kinds, although none but the best. Ah, but let me show you a side of fine pigskin I have just received! A beautiful leather, madam—and strong, strong as steel. I should say it is the very thing for your purpose."

He brought out the side of russet leather and smoothed it down on the counter.

"That will do very well," said Harriet, estimating its thickness with her finger.

Under her instructions, the man then took Richard's measurements for a wide folded belt and a pair of sleeves to strap over his forearms, the latter with spring-catches and rings at the wrist and elbow so they could be fastened together behind his back and then attached to other rings sewn into either side of the belt, thus rendering him quite helpless.

"There is one thing more," said Harriet, "but it is very important. Let me see a strip of your softest kid-skin in a matching shade. It must be about two feet long."

The man unrolled another piece of supple russet leather, and Harriet explained the purpose it was to serve. Richard, now blushing to the eyes, let the man take the measurement between his legs from the back of his waist to the front, and then note the precise situation of the pouch which was to confine and protect his genitals.

"An excellent thought, madam," the shopman murmured as he straightened up. "One sees the young gentleman is well looked after…"

Harriet smiled. "You will spare no expense for materials or finishing, of course. And be sure," she added, "to give the straps some extra length, so the harness cannot be outgrown. It must last for many years."

"Of course, madam, of course."

"Very well, I shall return for it at the end of the week. Come, Richard."

The man sprang to the door of the shop and bowed the customers out. As Richard passed, the craftsman winked at him with such a hideously sly satisfaction that the youth, already humiliated almost beyond bearing, was ready to sink through the floor.

CHAPTER FIVE

His face a little paler, his cheeks a little hollower than usual, Richard stole into Harriet's empty room. His governess had just gone out, leaving her pupil occupied with some schoolwork, which she had set him as a holiday task.

"You will not leave your room while I am gone," she had told him. "If you do, you will be whipped."

He obeyed the order at first. Then, despite the warning and the wholesome fear it implanted in him, he dared to leave his work table, open the door, and at last, drawn by his overmastering desire, to enter the bedroom filled with the subtle perfume of the young woman.

His heart was pounding with excitement. What had she just been doing there, he asked himself. He had no idea, could make no conjecture, but he was seized by an intense nervous disturbance at finding himself alone, for the first time, in this room where she lived and slept, this room haunted by the intoxicating fragrance of her clothing, her sachets, her body itself.

He approached the bed and shivered slightly. On the silk coverlet, beside the pillow, the governess had left a cane whose end was split and beginning to fray. That cane he knew only too well. The previous afternoon he had been whipped with it, as a punishment for his slovenliness in not having replaced a broken shoelace. His flesh was still tender from the effects of this correction, but the remembered sting of the rattan only intensified the ardor of his desire—that mysterious and uncertain desire that betrayed itself by an irrational wish to be mastered, scolded, shamed and whipped by his governess, and to touch and breathe the odor of every object belonging to her, above all, those consecrated to her most intimate use.

He picked up the cane with a trembling hand, and pressed his lips to the end that had felt her grip, imagining he could still detect the warmth and scent of the strong hand that had held it. Then, replacing the instrument of his torment, he let his gaze rove around the room. He was uneasy, oppressed, almost stifling, but the desire was stronger than everything else. Trembling in an excess of precaution, walking on tiptoe as if he feared to waken someone in the empty house, he made the circuit of the chamber.

All at once he stopped, riveted to the spot. On a low, straw-bottomed, high-backed chair whose form recalled that of a prie-dieu, a tiny handkerchief of fine batiste was lying, crushed almost flat. In front of the chair stood a pair of high-heeled shoes from which Harriet had changed before going out.

His throat was dry, his heart beating wildly, and

his penis now almost burst the cloth of his trousers. He bent over and knelt down, took the handkerchief and carried it to his lips. It exhaled a delicious perfume, the same he had breathed on that unforgettable evening when his governess had undressed in front of him before going to bed. And this handkerchief was at once crushed and flattened! Immediately he understood that in order to change her shoes Harriet had seated herself on this chair, and therefore on the handkerchief. The little square of batiste was thus doubly precious to him. He kissed it once more, long and passionately, and then hid it under his shirt, against his skin, against his heart. What delicious hours he would pass that night, he though, when he could bury his face in it, crush it against his taut testicles, wrap it around the head of his erected penis, and at last shoot his warm sperm with the thrill of anticipation.

But perhaps, even more than the handkerchief, the shoes attracted him. He picked them up, smelled them, covered them with such kisses as a lover would bestow on the body of an adored mistress. He stroked them tenderly, drew back the tongues and tried to kiss the inside. He gazed at them with love and reverence and pressed them passionately to his breast.

He felt in a confused manner the pointlessness, the madness of these endearments bestowed on inanimate objects. But then he began to ask himself if they were really so inanimate. He was dimly aware that there resided in this supple leather something more than the idea of the charming foot it had clasped, more than the sweet of intoxicating perfume it gave off. There was some immaterial essence that he was unable to explain and, though he did not conceive or clothe the idea in comprehensible terms, for him it was the symbol of an exquisite feminine domination.

At this point, absolutely unable to control himself, he opened his trousers, freed his rigid penis and began to masturbate. But the next moment, struck by an idea of marvellous simplicity and fitness, he slipped his member inside the shoe itself, drove it firmly into the pointed toe and began massaging and squeezing the soft leather from outside. The exquisite sensations he derived from this exercise were apparent in the nervous jerking of his hips as they unconsciously mimicked the genuine act of love. And now, quite careless of the consequences, he was about to ejaculate in the delicious leather prison itself, when a sound behind him chilled him to the marrow. He turned round and saw Harriet.

She was smiling, her thin lips parted in that terrible curve he knew so well.

As if stricken by paralysis, all the strength fleeing from his body as the blood gushed from an open wound, he could not move for an instant. He tried to unsheathe his member, but she halted him with a gesture.

"Stay as you are!" she said.

Deliberately she took off her bonnet and gloves and laid them on the dressing table. Then she approached the boy who, with the toe still fitted over his penis, his eyes wide with terror and entreaty, watched her coming toward him without a cry, word or a movement.

"So you are enjoying my shoes, sir!" she said in a low voice. She picked up the other shoe,. and, seizing his long hair in her fingers, rubbed the leather vigorously against his face, which swiftly became as red as fire. "So, you like my shoes!" she cried, her anger bursting forth. "That is what you like, is it? Put your hands behind you! Yes, behind you, I said. There now, kiss it. Kiss it again! You wretched boy! Again, again! Have you had enough of such vileness now?"

Her anger suddenly mastered her. Dropping the shoe, she slapped his cheek with all the strength of her arm. So hard was the blow that he would have fallen if she had not still held him upright by the hair. Deliberately, she slapped him again. "And now down with your trousers!" she cried. "Down with them you wretch! Ah, you like shoe leather, do you? You shall have it then!"

His head, ringing from the blows of her hand choked with sobs, his mouth sore and already swelling from the friction of the shoe, Richard fumbled desperately with his belt. The next moment his trousers slipped to the floor.

Harriet seized him and bent his unresisting body towards her, clasping his lowered head between her knees. The bare flesh of his buttocks, on whose ivory pallor faint signs of the previous day's caning were still visible, was stretched, taut and quivering, before her. Grasping her shoe by the heel, she began striking him with sharp blows of the smooth elastic sole.

The reports of leather on bare flesh continued for almost a minute, mingling with the muffled cries of the boy who, feeling suffocated by the pressure of the strong young knees, was nearly fainting with pain and terror.

Harriet, her face livid, her lips drawn back to show her small white teeth, had begun by striking with all her strength. But her anger, perfectly genuine, evoked by the evidences of the boy's perverted taste which was entirely at variance with her plans, gradually subsided. She experienced the sensual relief which such an exercise unfailingly brought her. By the time she had ceased, the boy's buttocks were a rich glowing scarlet and she had recovered herself completely.

Released from her grip, Richard crumpled to the thick carpet and lay there, his face in his hands, sobbing and gasping weakly.

She regarded him calmly for a few moments, then, with the point of her foot, she turned him over. Little by little, the sensuality of the punished boy was reaffirming itself now that his fright was receding. Harriet knitted her brows with determination. I shall have to take further measures, she thought.

"Get up, sir," she said. "And put your clothing in order. How dare you give such a vile display? Your shamelessness is revolting."

He rose and drew up his trousers. His cheeks were burning. He was filled with such a mingled sense of shame and unappeased desire that he could not meet his governess' eyes.

"Go to your room, undress yourself, and wait for me there," she said coldly. "I am not through with you yet, Richard."

He obeyed. No sooner had he taken off his clothes than Harriet entered his room. She was carrying the leather belt and sleeves she had ordered from the saddler. "I did not know we should have occasion for the whipping harness quite so soon, Richard," she said. "Indeed, I had hoped it would not be needed for a long time. But your conduct has shown me that I must take the most extreme measures. You have disappointed me more than I can say."

The note of reproach in her voice affected him even more than the prospect of further chastisement. A great sob of anguish rose in his breast, and falling on his knees before her he burst into tears. "Oh, ma'am, ma'am—I'm sorry," he stammered. "I—I couldn't help it. I'll never do it again! Only please, please don't be angry with me…"

"But I am no longer angry with you, Richard," she said calmly. "I am merely saddened to find such inclinations in you, and I am, more than ever, resolved to root them out. The whipping you are going to receive will be as much a corrective as a punishment of your wickedness. When it is all over you will be forgiven. Come now, get up and put on your harness!"

Under Harriet's direction he buckled the sleeves on his arms, girded himself with the belt and attached the strap that protected and confined his genitals.

"Very good," she said. "Now that you know how to put it on, I shall expect you to do so yourself whenever there is occasion for you to wear it in future. Turn around now, please…"

He obeyed. She drew his arms behind his back, folded them tightly, and snapped the catches in place.

Richard, feeling himself absolutely helpless, experienced a sudden emotion of panic. Breaking away sharply, he began to twist and strain against the straps, bending and writhing ineffectually, his face pale, a hunted look in his eyes.

Harriet watched his struggles with a detached and outwardly impassive air. She well knew the effects of such restraint, and congratulated herself on their success in further breaking her pupil's spirit. For a while, she followed his disordered movements without speaking. When they ceased and the boy stood crouched in front of her, panting and trembling, she began to smile.

"Come now. Richard," she said. "You see you must resign yourself. There is no use struggling any longer. You will only tire yourself to no purpose." She stepped forward and took him by the upper arm, supporting his body which suddenly became weak. "Lie down on your bed now. Very good. I shall leave you now, and I shall not come back until the evening. It is then that we will settle our accounts."

She pulled the coverlet over his trembling body and drew the heavy curtains. Then she turned away without another word and left the room, locking the door behind her.

For Richard, lying helpless in his bed, the hours until evening passed slowly. Outside, the world drowsed through the afternoon of a beautiful English summer day, the sunshine growing ever mellower and more golden as the sun moved lazily across a pure and cloudless heaven. It lingered and prolonged itself as if unwilling to leave the quiet country landscape. The hours rang out faintly from the priory church in the town, and they too seemed to be deliberately spacing themselves widely apart, in obedience to some timeless element of the day.

In the darkened bedroom of the house where the pinioned boy lay waiting, time seemed to have stopped altogether. Still tormented by a burning desire for something of which he had no conception, his imagination was tossed between thoughts of punishment and voluptuousness. They were prospects confused yet complementary, ideas inextricably entangled in a quivering, ambiguous sensibility whose only focus was in the image of the woman he loved. Indeed, he was prey to such closely mingled trepidation and desire that he seemed to be awaiting, in the arrival of his beloved, at once the signal of a martyrdom and an appeasement.

Ah, how many of us, looking back on our own childhood, might not say that we too have been consumed at some time by such a curious amalgam of emotion? And how many would not admit that in such hours of anguished expectation was forged, more strongly than ever, the sensual link that so mysteriously unites the ideas of pleasure and pain?

Harriet herself, perhaps, had known such an experience. Of such a possibility we cannot speak with certainty. But her understanding of the conditions under which the mind is at its most impressionable entitles us to say, at least, that she was a psychologist both profound and practical.

She entered the room so quietly that he had not even heard the rustle of the cape. The cool, pleasant voice startled him.

"Get up, Richard."

As he struggled off the bed and stood before her, he saw the mysterious leather martinet doubled in her hand.

"No," she said, as if reading his thoughts, "you will not have the strap tonight. But do not congratulate yourself too soon, my dear. I am sparing you a strapping only so that you may make a long and thorough acquaintance with this new martinet." She smiled, and shook out the heavy leather lashes in her hand. "I think you will find it is an instrument quite able to command your respect."

He gazed at her and shivered. More even than her anger, he had learned to dread this pleasant, almost quizzical air. She was never, he had found, more merciless than when in such a mood. As the beautiful bare arm swung the lashes through the air with a soft hissing sound, the muscles of his loins and thighs contracted involuntarily.

"Bend over, Richard."

He obeyed, hardly able to control the shaking of his knees as she stepped behind him.

The first blow drew a scream from him. The rounded, tapering thongs had seemed to cut into his buttocks like hot blades.

"Oh...miss! Please—I can't—I can't bear it!"

Harriet laughed. "Ah, you will have to bear it, Richard." She raised her arm and lashed him again, drawing another wild scream. "It stings, doesn't it? she said calmly. "It has a different sting, I dare say, than the sting of your wretched sensuality! Keep telling yourself that this good whip is driving out those evil inclinations, and be thankful for its virtue. Straighten your knees, please! We have just begun."

Very slowly, very methodically, the correction proceeded. Harriet was taking her time. He is really going to suffer tonight, she told herself, thrilling to the idea of his helplessness and her own power. Already her own sensuality was aroused, her cleft had begun to grow deliciously moist.

Richard had never before known such agony. Accustomed to the keen but superficial smart of strap and cane, he was receiving with terrified amazement the strokes of an instrument whose bite seemed to penetrate his entire loins, as if the thongs were literally tearing him to pieces. He tried to retain his bent position, to keep his knees stiff, to present his buttocks to his tormentress in the way she had so carefully trained him. But as the minutes went by, he found himself slowly weakening. It was not, he thought desperately, that his resolve was giving way, it was his limbs themselves that refused to obey him. His screams of agony no longer gave him any relief. He began swaying on his feet, his legs bending, his body involuntarily swinging from side to side.

"Richard!" said Harriet in a warning tone. "You are forgetting yourself. Do not make me angry with you, or you will regret it..."

"I—I can't help it," he gasped, straightening up and turning to her piteously. "I'm trying, ma'am..."

Harriet drew the lashes through her fingers as she looked at him with a cruel smile. "You must try a little harder then," she said. "Bend over properly now, keep your knees straight, and let us have no more of this foolishness. Your knees, sir, I said! Your knees!" She lashed him shrewdly in the tender hollows of his knees, and with a sharp scream he straightened his legs convulsively. "That is better," she said approvingly. "You will find it better to do as you are told."

She resumed the task of discipline with an appearance of calm. But, by now, she was deeply stirred. The blood had mounted to her head. Her breath was coming faster, the secretions poured ecstatically from her womb and bathed the passage and the very lips of her throbbing vulva. With her left hand she drew the folds of her cape tightly around her hips, feeling the contact of the material against her bare flesh, stiffening her spine voluptuously as if she were offering her own magnificent buttocks to some imaginary flagellant. She began to wield the lashes more swiftly.

But Richard had now reached the limit of his endurance. When his strength deserted him it did so suddenly, and he fell limply to the floor.

Harriet, as if balked at the moment before her goal, gave an exclamation of rage. "Get up!" she cried.

He struggled to his knees, but with his arms strapped behind him he could get no farther. And then, suddenly invaded by an immense and overpowering weakness, he crumpled to the floor once again, sobbing with pain and exhaustion.

"So you will not obey me?" she said, her voice almost stifled with suppressed fury. "So much the worse for you!"

She pulled the hood over her head. Richard, seeing the ominous gesture, gave a shriek of terror and closed his eyes. The next moment he felt the leather lashes cutting into him where he lay.

For the next minute the young governess seemed possessed by a demon. Stooped over her pupil's writhing body, she plied the whip with all her strength, bringing it down on whatever part of his flesh she could. Secure in the knowledge that the harness protected the boy's precious genitals from any injury, she was able to forget everything but her own crescendo of lust. Under her savage blows, he rolled and twisted helplessly on the carpet, his whole body doubling and straightening, his legs beating the floor, his pain and terror released in sounds like the insensate howling of an animal.

Then all at once the tall caped figure drew away from him. The martinet dropped from a nerveless hand. Her whole superb body, swaying and supporting itself against a heavy chair, began to tremble as long sensual shudders passed through it from head to foot. A great breath, half sob, half

117

groan, burst from her breast. Her loins jerked ecstatically, and her breathing prolonged itself into a profound and quivering sigh. She dropped into the chair, her hand pressed between her thighs as she coaxed the last vestiges of sensation from her screaming genitals.

Through the half darkness of the room, as if from far away, Richard's voice sounded, faint and almost strangled with sobs.

"Miss...Oh—is it all over—now?"

"Yes," said Harriet softly. "It is all over, Richard."

She rose and bent over him, unfastening his arms. "Get up now and come over here," she said.

With the release of his limbs, and hearing Harriet's tone of tenderness, he felt his fear passing away like a black cloud before a fresh and healing breeze. But more than this, added to his relief like some priceless pendant, he had heard a new note in his governess' voice, something carrying a different message than any ever before conveyed to him. It was a vibration in which he sensed the expression of a love deeper than any she had hitherto avowed, and with which was mingled the suggestion of some mysterious acknowledgement of some gratitude.

As she drew him gently onto her lap, he laid his head against her shoulder, and then, raising his lips to her ear, whispered through the folds of the little hood that still confined her hair, "Oh miss, miss. I love you, I love you."

Harriet tightened the embrace of her arm around the naked boy. In the darkness, her own lips, so recently curled and drawn back in all ferocity of her ardor, trembled slightly. "Yes," she said, in a voice she strove to render calm, "I am afraid

118

you care for me only too much, and in a way I must condemn." She felt the sudden throb that answered the pressure of her hand. "Richard," she said in a tone of warning.

He was seized by an uncontrollable trembling, filled once more with that mingled emotion of terror and desire. But it was the latter, now, that prevailed. "Oh, ma'am," he whispered, "I can't help it. Please, please don't be angry with me!"

Harriet drew a deep breath. But when she spoke her tone was calm and even. "Get up now, take off your harness and go to bed."

She remained seated while he obeyed. The room was now almost dark. Outside, the moon had risen above the treetops and was penetrating faintly through the curtains.

Lying on his back, the coverlet pulled up to his chin, Richard watched the tall, silent figure in the chair. Then he saw her rise, and standing erect draw the hood from her head. He saw the bare arm raised to the throat, and the next moment, with a splendid sinuous movement of the beautiful shoulders, the long cape was slipped off and fell in the chair behind her. Harriet was nude.

She stood for a moment in the center of the room, presenting to the boy on the bed a vision of such beauty that he was breathless with ecstasy. Then she advanced slowly. He could see her face now in the semi-darkness, grave and intent. But he had no eyes for anything but this magnificent body, which swam before him like that of some antique deity.

With a deliberate gesture she drew the coverlet below her hips, and sat down beside him on the bed. Once again, he felt the intoxicating pressure of her hand on his half-risen member.

119

The two nude figures, shadowy and indistinct in the dark bedroom, remained thus for a few instants. A shaft of moonlight, peering through the narrow opening in the curtains, fell on the motionless white bodies, illuminating them like marble, turning them to a statuary group at once tender and pagan. They were like a piece of sculpture in which was symbolized but one more variant of the ineffable aspiration of mankind, but one more aspect of that divine and multiform Eros who can do no wrong.

"Oh, miss," he whispered as he felt his member swelling under the touch of her fingers, "please...please don't punish me the way you did last time..."

"No," she said softly, "this time I will make you spend properly, Richard. Do not be frightened. Lie back, relax..."

Her hands began to move slowly, firmly, ringing the shaft and the bulb itself with a deep and satisfying friction, etching on the boy's affections a message never to be forgotten, a sensual memory, a type and pattern of voluptuousness to which he might turn back with longing for the rest of his life, as if it were the indelible imprint of herself. And as his orgasm was achieved, his hot puerile sperm gushing in short spasms into her strong hands for the first time, she leaned over and joined her parted lips to his, receiving like a viaticum the breath of his young rapture.

CHAPTER SIX

The regime initiated on that evening was continued at regular intervals throughout the holidays. Thus Richard, by turns scolded, beaten, and indulged, had his buttocks whipped to fiery heat and his orgasms induced by the skillful and persistent manipulations of the governess, and was obliged to undergo the succession of emotional states evoked by such treatment. He was raised to a condition of disturbance and excitation impossible to describe.

Harriet had also taken other measures to ensure her pupil's sense of dependence and inferiority. His schoolboy attire had been exchanged for a costume combining elements of the girlish and infantile. He wore a wide-sleeved blouse, short velveteen trousers, socks and low shoes. This dress, highly favorable as it was to the infliction of instant discipline, was devised by Harriet with the principal aim of heightening his self-consciousness in public.

This latter end was so well accomplished that whenever in the course of their walks together they met anyone on the roads or lanes, Richard was seized by a fit of shyness and sense of indignity such that he would flush and drop his eyes, quite unable to meet the gaze of persons he imagined were looking at him with either amusement or contempt. At such encounters he would feel that not only was his costume observed with ridicule, but also that the whip of cords his companion carried unobtrusively, doubled in her hand, furnished a further indication of his humiliating servitude.

But above all it was the other boys of his age whom he dreaded meeting in these rambles. Then, noting the jackets, breeches and boots of these carefree, sturdy youths, seeing the air of joyous freedom with which they roamed the beautiful wooded countryside, bearing the catapults, fishing-rods and other engines with which the tribe of youths wages a happy and unceasing war on the denizens of pond, tree and meadow—it was then that he would find himself thinking of their liberty with a sharp and wistful envy. They had no governess forever at their side, he would think. Their days were not passed in constant subjection to a woman, their waking and sleeping thoughts were not dominated by her menacing image, and their sexual amusements and very ejaculations were not conditioned by the cruel lash of a cane.

Indoors, the days went by in a constant round of minor corrections and humiliations. He wore the whipping harness almost continually. By evening, he would be in tears of pain and bewilderment. Often, driven to the limits of his emotional endurance, Richard sought a desperate relief in fits of silence and sullenness. It was then the governess, quick to note these signs of a raw and quivering sensibility, improved the occasion with all her vigor. These were the evenings when he was dismissed instantly to his room, there to await a repetition of those torments and raptures that were indeed the essential factors in his peculiar training.

By the middle of summer, his existence had become little more than an uninterrupted series of chastisements and deprivations, interspersed with the sensual indulgence through which the fixation of his interests and the corruption of his desires were being slowly and thoroughly carried out.

For her part, Harriet was experiencing a sense of accomplishment, almost of triumph. Outwardly calm, even cold, she was in reality filled with such joyful satisfaction that she had even to check the indulgence of a hope that seemed to be surpassing all her expectations. Never had she thought her pupil's sensibility would develop with such directness and precocity; never had she known a boy whose member had such powers of erection, endurance and recovery. Every day, too, she discovered fresh treasures in his mind and heart, and exulted almost with trepidation in the promise of those qualities she most valued in a man.

He will be as I wish him, she thought, trembling inwardly, and he will be mine. We will be happy, some day, as few persons are happy in this wretched world. A few years more, only a few years more, and the fruit will be ripe. Ah, what a heaven-directed chance it was that guided me to him, and that brought us to this place, this place where none can interfere, where no one even knows!

In this last supposition, however, she was not

entirely correct. Already word of Miss Marwood's disciplinary methods had gone forth into the neighborhood and the town itself, and not a few were aware that there was a young gentleman in the Lovel house who was being, as the saddler put it, "brought up by hand." This phrase had a more extended application than the saddler knew.

Molly, the caretaker's wife, had been the first to diffuse her tales of the lavish use of the strap and cane, tales that evoked the interest and admiration of her listeners. Many a mother, indeed, had nodded and tightened her lips in silent approval, and many a wife was impelled to a reverie into which we shall not inquire too closely.

Nor was auricular proof lacking of these tales, which soon spread over the entire countryside. Passers on the highroad at evening had heard and had paused to listen to the faint but unmistakable sounds coming from the house hidden by its walls and woods. Some shrugged indifferently, others merely laughed, but others, we know—and in this place we may avail ourselves of an author's omniscience—had been deeply stirred by these indications of a scene they could visualize only too clearly.

But these were not the only ears to receive the message of Harriet's severity. And we may ask ourselves what the governess would have thought had she known of her other hearers?

How should she know that behind the house, not far among the woods, a shady lane crept past the property of Mr. Lovel, a tree-embowered path known from time immemorial as Lover's Lane? And how should she have known that in this lane, in the very woods themselves, the youths and maidens of the countryside repaired for their rustic

courting? Many a young couple, couched on beds
of fern and bracken, heard the sounds of the whip
and the shrieks of the tormented boy, and turned
to handle, suck, and possess each other with an
ardor unaccountably renewed and sweetened by
that sombre litany floating on the evening air.

PART THREE
CHAPTER ONE

While the corruption of the boy was thus being successfully pushed forward, his father was making no less rapid advances in the agreeable science of debauchery. By now, indeed, Mr. Lovel had realized in what sphere his true happiness lay, that its focus was comprehended in the various openings of his mistress' body, and that the proper end of his existence was to ejaculate in them as often as possible.

Already the life of business had lost its charm for him. The attraction of making money now seemed inferior to that of spending it, the time spent in his office was but hours deducted from the time he spent in Kate's arms. As he himself said to his mistress, who was now permanently installed in the house on Great Portland Street, the thrill of successful speculation in the London Stock Exchange was nothing compared with the satisfaction of discharging his sperm in her mouth, her bowels, her womb, and her hands.

He had for some time now made up his mind to exchange the life of business for the life of pleasure, and residence in London for residence abroad. The day he made his final dispositions to this effect was for him the happiest he had known for many years.

That very evening he broke the news to Kate. They were lying in bed at the time, savouring the pleasant exhaustion ensuing on an act of love. Arthur had taken her from behind, dividing his attentions equally between the anus and vulva, and penetrating each in turn until he discharged. Then Kate began speaking of Richard.

"He and Miss Marwood will be coming back this very month," she said. "Perhaps you wish me to go live in my flat again."

"My dear Kate," laughed Arthur, "what could put such an idea in your head?"

"Nothing but common sense, Arthur. He is old enough that it will do the boy no good to be living in the same house with his father's whore. People would not like it. And I feel too that this governess does not much appreciate my being here. So, what with one thing and another, I shall feel a little cramped and uneasy, and I thought you might too."

Her protector's only answer was to take her in his arms and kiss her with the greatest tenderness, after which he made her sit up in bed and listen to the good news he had been saving for her.

"And so, my dearest girl," he finished, "we are leaving this gloomy great house and this wretched climate for ever. Does that not make you happy?"

Kate, who had been listening to him with both hands clasped in delight to the rosy nipples of her breasts, slipped out of bed and danced naked around the room, so great was her pleasure.

"Oh, Arthur my darling," she cried, "this is like a dream come true! I was so sad with thinking I might not lie with you night and day from now on, and now I am to be with you forever and always. We are to travel over Europe and see all the sights. Happy, Arthur? To be a woman running about all day with the man she loves and fucking with him all night? What more could a woman ask?"

Arthur looked at her tenderly. Already his genitals had begun to stiffen with reanimated desire.

"And oh," Kate went on, "we shall visit all the lovely whorehouses too, shall we not? For I have heard they have grand ones in Europe, and they have all kinds of machines and contrivances for increasing man's pleasure. I would like to study them so I may know how to give you the finest time and the greatest joy in spending of any man in the world." She paused, then sitting beside him she took his splendid member between her hands. "But what is to happen to poor Richard?"

"Why, poor Richard, as you call him, is a rich man as of today. I have settled half my fortune on him, with immediate enjoyment of the income, while the capital will be his as soon as he had reached his majority."

"Why, what a good father you are, Arthur!" exclaimed his mistress, bending down and impulsively kissing the rosy tip of his swelling penis. "And who have you made the trustee?"

Arthur laughed. "Who else but his own Miss Marwood? For though I don't care for her style at all, I've absolute confidence in her. She has a real head on her shoulders, and in spite of all her flogging of the boy she's devoted to him, as anyone can see. Yes, Kate, I feel this is the best thing for everyone concerned. Especially for myself. By this one stroke I rid myself of all family responsibility, I make some amends to Richard by making him a very wealthy young man, I secure his welfare by appointing Miss Marwood his trustee, I place her in a position of authority—and that is what that young woman wants above all, believe me!—and I assure myself a future of happiness with you, my dear Kate, a future without a care except that of multiplying our enjoyment of each other's society."

"And is all this done?"

"Signed, sealed, and delivered, my dear. We leave for Paris tomorrow night."

"Oh Arthur," she cried, "my heart is so full I cannot speak. But see, your prick is so fine and hard and proud now, and what shall I do with it? What would you like best? Should you like to bugger my arse again, my heart's darling?"

"No, Kate, I think I must fuck your mouth now, But we'll try something new. Lie down on you back. Now purse your lips, make that lovely mouth of yours as round and tight as your quim, and then hold still so that I can enjoy it at my own leisure."

Then, straddling her shoulders and supporting himself with his arms above her head, he pressed the glowing head of his superb penis to her protruding lips. He let it play against them tantalizingly for a few moments, and then inserted it slowly into the delicious wet cavern now transformed into a simulacrum of that other vent between her thighs.

"Ah," he said, moving his hips up and down and causing his member to slide in and out of the tight clinging orifice, "your mouth is as good to fuck as your vulva, Kate! Now knead my testicles a little, and tickle my hole with your finger. But not too much. I will take my time before I spend."

For the next few minutes he exercised his member in this leisurely way, by turns withdrawing it altogether and plunging it into the tight muscular ring of her firmly posed lips. Then, feeling the sperm gathering at the root of his shaft and the preliminary thrill of the crisis threading his loins, he thrust deeply within her mouth and ceased his movements.

"Now, now, Kate," he whispered: "now use your tongue. Suck me right out, to the last drop!" And the next moment he was shuddering in the throes of an exquisitely prolonged orgasm as the greedy muscles of his mistress' tongue and glottis slowly drew the hot sperm from the very base of his member to the bulb, milking it like the most passionate vulva, making it jet into her throat where it was voluptuously tasted and swallowed.

He remained with hips resting on her face and his subsiding member lodged in the warm embrace of her mouth for a long time, savouring the perfection of his orgasm. Then he withdrew, bent over and kissed his mistress' forehead with the greatest tenderness.

"Well, Kate," he said, "I have heard the whores in France and Italy highly praised for their ability to give a man pleasure, but I will back you in a contest with any of them, at any time! Indeed, I think my own Irish whore is on all counts the best in the world!"

❖ ❖ ❖

Thus it was that when Harriet and Richard arrived in London a week later on a cold, wet evening in September, they found the house on Great Portland Street empty save for Bridget, who handed the governess a letter in which Mr. Lovel acquainted her with his decisions and how he had put them into effect.

Harrier remained motionless for a full minute, digesting the full import of the news, which surpassed all her wildest expectations. At last she handed the letter to Richard, and watched him closely while he read it.

"So you see, my dear boy," she said, "that while you are now a young man of fortune you remain, nonetheless, under my absolute authority. I warn you that I shall keep the same tight rein over you during the two years of my stewardship as I have done in the past." She smiled suddenly. "Well, does the idea appeal to you?"

He raised his eyes to hers timidly, but she could not mistake the happiness and adoration in the dark-blue gaze. "Oh yes, ma'am," he whispered. "You know, I shall always be happy while you are with me—always…"

She took his face between her hands. "Even though I am still your master and hold you in check, Richard? Allow you no freedom? Whip you without mercy, and humiliate you in the face of the world? Even then, Richard?"

He lifted his face, seeking her lips. "Oh yes, miss," he whispered. "Even with all that, I shall love you and be happy."

She pressed her mouth to his passionately. Her triumph knew no bounds, her heart was beating swiftly. Against her thighs she felt the tremendous swelling of his boyish member. She passed her hand swiftly between his legs, thrilling at the contact with this unfailing index of his sensuality.

"Thank you," she said softly. "And now as a reward for your admission, you will go upstairs and to bed right now. I will come and relieve your sexual tension later. Remember to behave yourself until I do."

CHAPTER TWO

Thus a year went by, and Richard was more in thrall to his governess than ever. For by this time he was so dependent on her caresses that he could not do without them.

This condition had been brought about by Harriet's consistent and persevering regime of corruption. Thanks to her methods, the boy had been led to so intimate an association between the ideas of self-indulgence and corporal suffering that he was no longer able to effect an erection, much less an orgasm, by his own efforts. No sooner did he touch his genitals than the remembered menace of the cane filled his consciousness and paralyzed his nerves, his flesh shrank and his desire subsided. There was for him now only one means of incitement and gratification, and that was literally in his governess' hands.

Harriet had, in fact, kept her promise to Mr. Lovel. Richard was cured of the puerile habit that had constituted such a bar to his health and happiness. The fact that he was no less a slave to a woman's manipulations was, she felt, a distinct advance for him. The circumstance that this enslavement of his mind and senses fell in with her own plans seemed to her only a further proof that all was going well.

Nonetheless, encouraged as she was by the obvious success of her grand strategy, she felt it was time for a change of tactics.

It was now drawing towards the end of winter. During the past months she had whipped and gratified him with such freedom that the whole area of his loins was in a condition of extraordinary co-suggestibility. Accordingly, she determined to cease these attentions and leave his emotions to ferment of themselves.

"Richard," she said, "I think it is now time you acquired the habit of study by yourself. You have made excellent progress so far under my supervision, and now we must see what you can do alone. I will map out your course of study, and that is all. And this is not the only sphere in which I wish you to show some signs of manly independence. You are now old enough to do without the relief in which I have indulged you for so long, and you must become accustomed to abstinence and restraint."

He said nothing. His dismay left him no words. He could merely look at her with a dumb appeal that bespoke only too well his sense of deprivation.

During the following week he was left entirely to himself.

The experience was devastating. Apprehensive by disposition, rendered constitutionally unsure of himself by the neglect he had suffered during his childhood, he was all too prone to let his imagination run riot among his fears. As the days and weeks went by and Harriet preserved her air of silence and aloofness, only seeing him at meals and for a few minutes in the evening, his fancy presented to him, in constantly more vivid colors, the picture of that situation he dreaded above everything else in the world—the withdrawal of his governess' love. Indeed, so great was his distress that the lack of sexual gratification was quite reduced in the scale of his suffering. He missed her caresses, but it was her darling companionship that he missed most of all.

His studies suffered along with his spirits. Obliged to sit alone in the schoolroom day after winter day, he found he could not concentrate on work of any kind. The hours were spent in interminable sessions of melancholy and fruitless reveries. But the careless and inadequate way in which he followed the schedule laid down for him by Harriet went now unnoticed. No longer was his idleness requited by instant and vigorous punishment, and this, simply as an indication of his altered and forgotten status, was something he now came to miss. He had lost interest and significance, he felt, in the eyes of the woman he loved with all his heart.

Harriet observed him carefully and his unhappiness pleased her. But as the weeks went by, she realized that she had not foreseen her own reactions in the face of this mutual deprivation. Her own sensuality, accustomed to being gratified or at least initiated by the infliction of pain and the consciousness of power, was now cut off from its only source of satisfaction, and she began to wait with impatience the period when she had decided to resume her habits of severity.

At least, she told herself, I have shown him his utter subservience to me. But the last few days of this regime of separation were almost as painful for her as for the boy.

Entering the schoolroom quietly, she found Richard sitting in his accustomed place, his elbows leaning on the table, his gaze fixed idly on the rain-streaked window.

"Well, Richard," she said pleasantly, "I have come to see how you are getting on with your studies."

He wheeled in his chair at the sound of her voice. Now, with a strange shock of joy, he felt her arms once more passed affectionately around his shoulders as she sat beside him in the old familiar way.

His head whirled; he felt a wild surge of relief and desire. He stammered out a few words, feeling for a moment close to tears.

Harriet noticed his perturbation with a satisfaction she carefully concealed. But then, all at once, she herself was surprised, in her turn, by the emotion kindled in her by her pupil's glance of adoration. She controlled herself, resuming with a real effort her calm, impersonal air towards this handsome youth whose eyes were glowing with the beauty of unconscious, disinterested love.

But as her arm pressed his shoulder briefly, they both trembled with a peculiar awareness. In an instant the governess was on her guard. She moved her chair away from his, picked up a history textbook, and leafed through it rapidly, calming her agitation as she mechanically sought the chapter at which they had left off a month ago.

"We had reached the opening of the War of the Spanish Succession, had we not?" she asked evenly.

"Yes, miss," he said automatically. But he did not know what he was saying. All his attention was centered on the beautiful face which confronted him above the book in the well-known way.

She closed the book, her finger marking the place, and sat back. "This war was the consequence of conflicting claims to the throne of Spain, as you know. Now, tell me the names of those claimants, please." She glanced away at the window, and waited.

Richard had hardly heard the question. A strange lassitude filled him, his head was reeling, he could do nothing but gaze in fascination at his governess. His awareness of her physical presence, the fact that she was once more beside him, left no room in his brain for anything else.

She turned and met once again the pure ardor of his gaze, the worship expressed in his whole face. She saw the full boyish mouth, half open, trembling as if with an imminent avowal of love. She felt a suddenly renewed weakness in her own limbs, and summoned all her strength to her aid.

"I will refresh your memory," she said. "The claimants were three in number—the French Dauphin, the Elector of Bavaria, and the Emperor of Austria. Well, which of these claims did Britain support?"

The cold glance she managed to turn on him brought the youth to himself. He blushed and hung his head, his fingers twisting nervously.

"Which of—of these claims..." he repeated

stupidly, raking his memory, which refused to function at all.

"That is what I said."

"Why—why, it was the Dauphin, ma'am," he said, making a guess. "Was it not?"

"Idiot!" said Harriet, closing the book sharply.

Faced now with the fear and confusion of the youth before her, observing the awkward, embarrassed air that had taken the place of his look of romantic admiration and love, she had recovered herself completely, Her desires swung back to the region of cruelty and domination. Ah, she thought luxuriously, now for the relief of whipping!

Richard saw her rise silently, lay the book on the table, and move toward the cabinet in the corner. He heard the sharp click of the lock as she opened it, and then the soft, suggestive whistle of the cane in her hand.

"We will see what a good cane will do for your memory, Richard," she said. "Stand up! And hold out your hand, please."

He obeyed, trembling. She faced him, her eyes glowing and intent, tapping her palm lightly with the supple reed. "You have still another chance to answer my question," she said.

He stared at her helplessly. He had forgotten even what the question had been.

"Very well," she said, raising the cane slowly. The next instant she had lashed his palm with such force that he cried out. Her own eyes dilated slightly.

"That is not an answer, Richard," she said quietly. "Come, I am still waiting."

"Miss, I —"

The cane descended again, drawing another cry.

"You are trifling with me, Richard," she said.

"You know that I do not permit that. Be silent! Do not try to interrupt me. I am going to flog that hand of yours until you answer. Do you understand?"

"Yes, miss! But—but I don't know the answer!"

"Ridiculous! You are being willful, sir."

"No, no, miss! Please, I really—"

"Enough!" She cut his palm again with all the strength of her wrist. "Answer me. Ah, you will not, then? We shall see. Keep your hand up. Higher, please…"

At the twentieth stroke Harriet paused, savouring the pleasant glow diffused in her by this physical exercise, a warmth marched by the delicious sense of well-being brought her by the indulgence of her special tastes. She breathed deeply, luxuriously, feeling the sensual current flowing once again through her brain and body, bringing them the refreshment they had lacked for so long. Her eyes were shinning, there was a smile on her full lips.

"You are very obstinate, Richard," she said pleasantly. "Will you have a little more? There is still your other hand, you know, when I have finished with this one."

"Oh, no! Please, please, miss…no more! Let me explain…" His voice was choked with sobs. He could barely speak.

"Oh? Speak up, then. No, do not lower your hand, sir!"

"Please, miss, I—I've—"

"Speak up, I said. At once!" Calmly, deliberately, she lashed his quivering, swollen palm again. "What is it, Richard?"

"I've—I've forgotten the question, miss. No! Please, no more!" Wild with pain, he fell on his knees before her, reaching for her disengaged hand.

Harriet lowered her cane, drinking in the abject accents of his voice, thrilling to their renewed confession of her absolute power over his will and his flesh. "Indeed," she said quietly. "Then it appears you have been wasting my time. Get up at once, sir, from that ridiculous position. Stand up! Come here, and put your hands behind you."

She sank into the leather armchair, watching him as he scrambled to his feet and stood in front of her. For almost a minute she was silent, surveying his trembling form and downcast eyes. The sight of his distress and uncertainty was so exquisite that she prolonged the pleasure of watching him. It was by now incorporated in the melting softness of her vulva.

But Richard was far from being as miserable as he appeared. Even as he stood before his governess, in all the painful uncertainty of what might be coming, his heart was filled to overflowing with a tremulous hope. He felt a restoration of the trust he had always placed in her. A vague anticipation of happiness reawakened in him and was able to subsist, now, merely on the fact of her presence in the same room with him.

She has not forgotten me, he was thinking. She is still concerned over me. And she is here with me again! Oh, I would rather she whipped me, a dozen times a day even, than leave me to myself...

He raised his eyes to her face. "M-miss," he stammered in a low voice. "If you would—would ask me the question again, I will try to do better..."

Surprised, Harriet looked at him closely, endeavoring to read his mind. He is trying to escape his punishment, she thought. He is hoping I will only use the cane.

She surveyed him silently for a few moments longer before replying. "No, Richard," she said at last. "We are finished with our schoolwork this afternoon. I have seen enough to know that you have been idle all this past month—disgracefully, shamefully idle. The rest of this afternoon, Richard, will be devoted to punishment. You understand, of course, what that means?"

"Yes, miss," he mumbled. Hanging his head, he shifted awkwardly from one foot to the other.

"Then what are you waiting for?" she said sharply. "Prepare yourself at once!"

"Oh yes, miss..." He began fumbling at his waist. "I'm sorry—" With a swift movement of his hips, he let his clothing fall to the floor.

Harriet drew a deep breath as she saw his bare swelling buttocks. "Now bend over," she said. "Hands on your knees. Very good."

She rose and moved behind him, making the cane whistle in her gasp. "First of all," she said, "I am going to give you thirty strokes with the cane. That will be your punishment for trifling with me. Do you understand?"

"Yes, miss."

"After that, we will see."

She tapped his loins lightly with the cane, observing the shiver that went through him and the involuntary contraction of his muscles. And then, suddenly, the sight of the smooth, rounded flesh bared so submissively before her, the thought of how soon it would be dancing and quivering under the steady lash of the rattan, made her catch her breath in savage joy. Casting aside all thought of a preliminary lecture, simply unable to wait any longer, she drew back her arm and cut into him vigorously.

At the tenth stroke she stopped and stepped back.

"We shall take our time, Richard," she said coolly. "There is the whole afternoon before us, you know. And I wish to impress thoroughly on you the sense of your willful behavior while I caned your hand. You will find that such deceit does not pay. And now, there is something else about which I wish to speak to you. Stay as you are, please." She laid down the cane and came around to face him. "Hold up your head, sir! Look at me! I am speaking to you. Do you hear me?"

"Yes, miss."

"Then do not hang your head like that, please. Look at me, I said!"

He raised his swimming eyes to the gaze which was bent on him. "Yes, miss," he said abjectly.

"Very good. That is the kind of glance I like to receive from you at all times. At all times! Understand, Richard, I will not allow you to look at me as you did earlier this afternoon. You have become most insolent since I relaxed my authority over you. How dare you look at me like that? How dare you?"

"Miss, I'm sorry. Please, I—I meant no harm."

"Indeed. Then you have a very poor command of your features. Do you know, Richard, how a well-bred woman deals with such a look as you gave me when I first came in? Do you?"

"N—no, miss..."

"Hold up your head, sir! And look at me. I am speaking to you as a woman now, not as your governess. This is the answer to such insolence from a boy."

And before she had ceased speaking she had
slapped his face with stinging force—once, twice,
three times. His eyes saw stars, his cheek felt on
fire. Sick with shame and hurt, aghast at the realization of his governess' sense of injury, of her
interpretation of his boundless worship of her, he
hid his face in his hands and burst into tears.

"That is better, Richard," she said after a few
moments. "You are better like that. Stand up
straight, and take your hands from your face. You
have received the penalty of your insolence. Now,
now, you are forgiven."

With a sensation of absolute incredulity, he felt
her take his head between her two hands, he saw
the beautiful, beloved face approach his, and he
received with rapture the contact of her warm lips
pressed firmly to his own.

"You must learn to behave yourself with me,
Richard," she said coolly, drawing away from him.

Thus, by the time the afternoon was over, the
old relationship between governess and pupil had
been re-established. For Harriet, it was now free
from that troubling element of physical attraction
to which she had let herself succumb for a few
moments. Her womanly weakness was conquered,
and she had reasserted herself in the role of her
choice. For her, Richard had become once again
the submissive chattel, the minister to her stern
sensuality, a creature to be at once loved and
despised.

For his own part, Richard felt himself restored
to life, drawn out of that limbo of non-being in
which he had existed without her. The very severity she had shown him was the certain indication of
her regard, the assurance of his not being indifferent to her, the guarantee, even, of her love. His

chains, the chains in which he wished to live for the rest of his life, were more firmly riveted on him than ever. As in the past, he asked nothing of this young woman except that she should acknowledge his existence. By a caress or a blow, it made no difference.

CHAPTER THREE

Now that she was assured of Richard's entire devotion, Harriet might have been tempted to relax her vigilance and determination. But she realized that her greatest trial still lay before her. His love must be transformed into an active desire for her body. At the same time she must not yield to him, for any premature liberty she allowed him would be fatal to all her plans.

It was the prospect of residence at Christchurch that disturbed her most of all. There, in the surroundings where she had first learned to love her pupil, she knew she was particularly vulnerable to his charm and to her own feelings. Even now, seeing him every day, observing the increase in his beauty, she was tormented by the wish to enjoy his body to the utmost, to feel that exquisite member she had so often caressed, penetrating her womb. Her baffled sensuality found its only outlet in subjecting him to repeated acts of severity and humiliation.

When they arrived in Christchurch that summer her nerves were in a state of exacerbation. She was in fact in that condition, so dangerous to women, of wishing at once to tantalize and reject the man of her choice. While knowing the danger, she could not resist deliberately inciting him to the kind of behavior she both craved and feared.

The summer went by before she was impelled to bring matters to a head. For not until then had she felt sufficiently mistress of herself to hazard the experiment of directing her pupil's desires into the wished-for channel, an experiment she prefaced by refusing him all gratifications for a week.

For Richard, the sequence of events was an enigma from beginning to end.

That evening at dinner he had been conscious of an air of tension between them. Harriet said little, but he felt her fine eyes resting on him from time to time. It seemed her glance held some special message, some obscure promise he did not dare to formulate to himself. He was nervous and lacked appetite, and when dinner was finished he found himself still more at ease. He was suddenly aware that his feelings for the past hour had reproduced the trepidation so often experienced in this house in past years, when it had been a question of his submitting to some punishment of special sharpness during the hours preceding his bedtime.

"It is a fine evening," said Harriet. "Come, let us take a turn or two in the garden."

As he stood behind her to place the long cloak over her shoulders, he felt her incline against him, and saw her face turned back to him for an instant over her shoulder. Overcome by the contact, he put his arms around her and pressed her to him tenderly. She made no resistance for a moment or two, suffering his embrace with a passive tranquility. Then she drew away without a word and put her arm in his. As they passed into the garden she said in a low voice, "Be careful, Richard."

His only reply was to clasp her arm a little more closely. She did not relax or withdraw, merely saying, "I have told you to be careful. You will please do as I say."

His senses in a turmoil, his brain utterly confused, he walked on beside her, feeling the soft pressure of her arm and the occasional contact of her hip. Without knowing to do or say, he was conscious of nothing but the current of emotion running through him.

It was a dark, moonless night. The air was already soft with the fullness of summer and the odor of the mown fields. In the distance, crickets were singing. They reached the deeper shadow thrown by the woods, and Harriet suddenly paused and turned to confront him. He saw her face, no more than a white blur in the darkness, level with his own. He had the impression she was smiling. Then he felt her hands on his shoulders. His arms went around her, and their lips met.

A moment later he realized with a shock of shame and dismay the intrusion of another element in the pressure of his body against hers, and felt her drawing away. All at once the weight of her hands on his shoulders became more insistent, and in obedience to their pressure he sank to his knees before her, his arms still enlacing her, his head seeking the cleft of her knees. "Miss," he whispered, "forgive me."

She made no reply, her pose remained rigid. When he felt her hands leave his shoulders he raised his face fearfully to gaze at her. What he saw affected him like an electric shock. Her hands were raising the hood of her cloak, with the same gesture that had so often filled him with terror during his boyhood. Involuntarily he gave a little moan of fear and relaxed his grasp.

"Why, what is the matter, Richard?"

He stammered an inaudible reply, then buried his face once more in the folds of her cloak, trying to conceal his agitation. He heard her laughing softly.

"Ah yes," she said, "I understand. What a memory you have for little things, my dear! But there is no cause for alarm this time. I am hooding myself against the night air, you know." Unseen to him, her lips were curving in a triumphant smile.

"Come," she said at last. "We will go to bed. It is early yet, but I am tired. You will read to me for a while when I am in bed, just as you used to do in the old days. Do you remember?"

Indeed, he remembered only too well those troubling occasions!

The bedroom was dim, lit only by a heavily shaded lamp that extended the shadows of this luxurious room and caught up a thousand points of light from polished woods and ornaments of brass. The air was warm and humid.

Harriet waved him to the divan. "Sit here, Richard," she said. Then, deliberately, she began to undress.

The old familiar ritual, re-enacted before him now after so many months, affected him still more powerfully than it had when he was a boy. His

153

throat dry, his face burning, he followed the leisurely and graceful movements of the young woman in a fever of anticipation. Once more, he watched the methodical removal of gown, stays and linen. He heard the rustling of silks and taffetas. He smelled the warm odors being released in the room, each more intimate than the last. At last Harriet was clad in nothing but her shift. His eyes wavered and dropped.

"Richard," came her clear, cool voice. "Bring me my nightdress from the press, if you please."

He rose, opened the press, and saw the long silk garment hanging before him. With trembling hands he took it out and turned back to her. Then he stopped, transfixed.

Harriet stood nude before him, a faint smile on her lips. He gasped and lowered his eyes, unable to move.

"Well, my dear," she said. "What are you waiting for? One would think you had never seen me before."

He summoned up his courage, and looked full at her. Once he had done so he could not take his eyes away. His gaze devoured the magnificent contours of her neck, her breasts, her thighs, and he felt his breath almost stifling him. He moved blindly forward and took her in his arms. For a moment her mouth was turned to his, and he felt her whole body responding to the contact of his own. But when she drew away his arms dropped helplessly. He saw her smiling at him indulgently.

"Why, Richard," she said, "it is not yet time for you to kiss me tonight. We are not going to bed right away. And I have not yet done my hair. Wait where you are for a minute." And turning from him she sat down before the low mirrored dressing-table and began unfastening the masses of her hair.

Spellbound, he watched the movements of her beautiful arms as Harriet pulled the long ebony-backed brush over her tresses. He saw the serpentine undulation of her splendid back, and in the mirror caught glimpses of her large prominent breasts, centered by their tips of dark rose, which swam and quivered with the movements of her arm. A sob of desire rose in his throat, and he stepped forward and knelt behind her, his arms embracing her waist, his hands closing upon those treasures of her bosom, his mouth buried in the soft nape of her neck.

"Richard, this is too much!"

She had broke from him and rose, glaring at him angrily. "This behavior is disgraceful!"

"It's only that I love you—so much..."

Her brows drew together over her shining eyes. "You are impertinent, Richard." She paused, looking at him fixedly for a few moments. When she spoke again her voice was calm and level. "Come here and kneel down, sir."

She sat down and crossed her beautiful naked legs. Then, with one hand supporting her bare breast, she went on gravely. "Your conduct lately has led me to consider your condition very carefully. And I see that your temperament is altogether too passionate, too ardent. Until lately, I have been able to hold your passions in check by certain indulgences. But that must not continue. You will soon be a man, and you are too old to resort to that form of relief. No, my dear, there is only one course of action to be taken with you. You must be married."

He stared at her in astonishment. "Married?" he repeated stupidly.

"Yes, Richard, you must be married—to some

woman who will keep you in proper order."

"But I don't wish to be married. I—"

Harriet's brows drew together sharply. "Then you must control yourself. Do you understand?"

He noted the sudden lift and quiver of her breasts, and dropped his eyes. "Yes—but really, I don't wish to marry. I just want to live this way with you—forever…"

She looked at him quizzically. "You may feel more inclined for marriage after you have a few more months of chastity," she said, as she caressed her breasts idly. "Perhaps that will make you more receptive to some nice girl."

"Oh, but I don't want a girl!" His dismay was almost comic. "I want only you…"

Harriet's heart leapt. She felt her cheeks flushing. But when she spoke her voice was suddenly harsh.

"What do you mean!" she said. "How dare you address me in that way? Richard, if you ever do so again, if you ever suggest that I become your mistress, I shall whip you till blood comes. Do you understand?"

He reached blindly for her head. "Miss!" he cried in utter dismay, "I did not mean to suggest anything like that. Oh, believe me! I would not dare—I had never thought—"

"Then you must be careful how you choose your words. Get up now. Hand me my nightdress, and turn down my bed."

He obeyed, watching her tremulously as she slipped on the long white garment, drew its silk sash around her waist, and got into bed. When she spoke again her voice was once more cool and pleasant.

"Before you begin reading to me, there is something I should like you to see." She smiled, and adjusted the pillow behind her beautiful head. "Last winter in London I made a purchase especially for you. You will find it on the cabinet. Bring it to me, please."

As his eyes fell on the instrument on the cabinet his heart gave a sudden leap. He drew a short, deep breath. It was a thin, curling whip of black Russian leather.

"Yes," Harriet murmured, "You see, I was thinking of you even then. Well, what do you think of your new whip, Richard? Do you think it will help you to behave better? Bring it here to me, I said."

Trembling with a peculiar emotion, he picked up the whip, noting its lightness and balance. Little more than two feet in length, with a stiff handle that gradually became supple and tapered off to a fine threaded lash, it combined the features of a dog-whip and a lady's riding-whip. The sheen of the leather and the silver mounting gave to its cruel lines an air of distinction and elegance. He handed it to her silently.

"Thank you. I see you have nothing to say about it. Possibly your opinion on its merits has yet to be formed." She looked at him shrewdly, taking in the glance with which he devoured the whip before handing it to her.

He had been immediately fascinated by it. More than the strap or the cane, more even than her shoes, it seemed to sum up and symbolize his serfdom to Harriet more cogently than anything else. Now, as he watched her slowly draw the supple black lash through her fingers, he was seized once more by the opposed but complementary emotions of fear and longing. It was as if he already realized that to be beaten by this superbly cruel instrument would be a crowning experience in which pain and pleasure might be combined as never before.

Harriet laid it softly on her bedside table. "You would like to have a taste of it some time, would you not?" she said suddenly.

Shaken by an overmastering excitement, he met her piercing, clairvoyant gaze for an instant. "Yes, miss," he whispered breathlessly. "Oh, yes…"

Harriet's eyes flickered strangely, and her face flushed. Then she lay back in bed, still looking at him intently, concealing her triumph under a sudden change of demeanor.

"I am glad of that," she said. "It shows you are sensible of your needs—and of mine too. And in return for your admission I will allow you a privilege I have had in mind for you for some time, and to which your age really entitles you." She paused. "From now on, when we are alone together, you may address me by my first name, Richard. In public, of course, you will continue to call me Miss. But in private, as we are now, I shall be addressed as Harriet. Do you understand?"

"Oh, yes," he breathed. "Yes, Harriet." Never, he thought, had a sweeter sound passed his lips.

She gazed at him for a few moments, dissembling her own emotion at hearing for the first time the syllables of her name on the lips of the youth she loved.

"And now," she said, "take up that book and read to me, please."

He opened the book and began. Unaware of what he was reading, with his lips automatically framing the words before him, he was occupied simply with his own emotions, with his remembrance of the look she had just given him—in which he had seen the promise of a consummation.

Harriet's eyes gradually closed. Each time

Richard turned a page he stole a glimpse at the beloved face that had never seemed so beautiful as now, in this moment when he could watch it unobserved. His voice began to falter, his throat becoming dry as he grew sick with desire for this magnificent creature lying before him. He ceased reading and devoured with burning glances her face, her breasts, the outline of her lips beneath the thin coverlet. He dropped the book and stretched out his hands towards her.

"Richard, it is time you were in bed." Harriet's voice came softly, arresting him. She had opened her eyes and was gazing at him as if through a film of slumber.

"Yes, Harriet. Shall I kiss you goodnight?"

"No, you have done so already. Good night, dear boy."

"Harriet," he murmured, not rising.

"Yes, I know, Richard. It will not be long. Listen, my dear; leave the door of your room open. Do you understand?"

"Yes."

"Go now."

He rose and left the room, gaining his own in a fever of desire, anticipation and uncertainty. He undressed, and slipped nude between the sheets, his heart beating violently.

It was only towards dawn that he fell asleep, awaiting her all the while. She did not come.

CHAPTER FOUR

For the next two weeks, until the time came to leave the house at Christchurch, Harriet contrived to keep her enamored pupil in the same continual suspense and uncertainty. All that could be done to fire his ardor, by melting looks, chance contacts and caresses, was performed by her with ruthless generalship. As often as he stopped to the lure he was rebuffed, mocked, and turned away with a shrewd mixture of friendliness and disdain. He was left poised between hope and despair, between a half-awakened consciousness of his own attraction and a constant doubt of her feeling, but always in a state of sensual excitement.

He would have been astonished to know that she herself was in a condition approximating his own. But her energies were bent as much on concealing her desires as on resisting them, and he knew nothing of the torments she endured every night in bed, of the temptations she withstood. He

162

knew nothing of the long and exhausting frictions of her clitoris to which she had recourse but which left her in a state rather of fatigue than of satisfaction—still plagued by her erethism and already foreseeing the time when such practices would be no more effective for her than they were for Richard.

When they returned to London that September the autumn rains had already begun. As their cab rolled along the teeming streets whose lamps were reflected in the grimy water of drains and gutters, the tall houses of the great dark city seemed to be weeping tears of soot. Passing through the squalid district of Cirencester Place and Great Titchfield Street on their way from the station, they saw on all sides the evidences of poverty and vice—things that meant absolutely nothing to the boy but which filled the governess, as always, with repulsion and anger. A pair of street walkers, trailing bedraggled finery along the pavement, stopped and cried out to the two occupants of the cab as it slowed down at the corner of Clipstone Street.

"What did those women want, Harriet?" asked Richard naively.

Her eyes flashed. "I would not care to say. But I know what they should have, and what you should have too for asking such a question! Be silent, please."

Already depressed by the long train journey and the chill bleakness of London, and with his spirits still further lowered by his companion's stern and frigid air since that morning, Richard winced and shrank back in his seat, feeling now utterly miserable.

For a whole week his passion rose steadily. He was now obsessed by the idea of possessing his governess. The seeming impossibility of this outrageous ambition threw him into a kind of gloomy desperation. Every afternoon he walked the streets listlessly. Never, he thought, had the city been more dismal, the passers-by more drab and forlorn. His feet merely obeyed the impulse of a leaden mood that drove him to keep in motion like an animal on a treadmill.

During this time, he thought at intervals of her verdict as to the necessity of his being married. He recalled her actual words: "A woman who would keep you in order," she had said. But that would mean someone to take her place, and he wanted no one but her. On occasions another idea flashed before him, but he put it aside immediately. It was an impossible solution, one that had the air of something forbidden, almost the air of incest. And yet the idea kept returning to him, unbidden, still unformulated, but exciting and ever frightening with its promise of an undreamed-of happiness.

It was at night, however, that his distress mounted to fever pitch. Then, in the warmth and lamplit intimacy of the house, he would be driven almost to madness by the discrepancy between its proffer of intimacy and the dreary truth of his inability to compass his desires. The ritual of their "good nights" was the worst ordeal of all, a bitter mockery of assuagement in which he underwent the visit she paid to his bedroom, the soft embrace of her arms, the clinging warmth of her kiss.

One evening, when she had just taken her lips from his and was preparing to go, he burst into a storm of tears. With a gesture of abandon and despair, he pulled down the covers from his naked body, displaying his rigid member.

"Oh," he cried pitifully, "please, please, Harriet.

164

Will you not help me—just this once, oh, please?"

Seeing his marvellous glowing nudity, this prof-fered flesh centered by the urgently erected penis, she turned pale for an instant. She would have liked to throw herself on him in that very moment, to caress and guide this exquisite shaft into the whirlpool of her womb, and to let her whole being dissolve in the bliss of union. His breathing deep-ened, her eyes filmed over, but on the very brink of capitulation she drew back with a superhuman effort.

"Why, Richard," she said with an appearance of coldness that struck him to the heart. "Not only are you childish, you are becoming quite indecent. I have told you already you are much too old for me to occupy myself with your genitals. Those days are past."

He looked at her in absolute despair. "Then—then what shall I do? Harriet, what shall I do?"

In spite of her disturbance she was able to smile at his tone and attitude. "You must remember what I told you. You must marry."

"But whom shall I marry?"

"Ah," she shrugged, "you must decide that for yourself. But you should decide soon."

"Soon?" His voice was agonized.

She looked at him coolly. "Yes. It is only a week now until you reach your majority and come into your fortune. My duties as trustee will be finished. You must decide on the kind of life you mean to lead."

"I only wish to spend the rest of my life with you, Harriet..."

"That is impossible."

"But why?"

She laughed shortly. "You idiot, I will soon no longer be your governess or the trustee of your estate. I will have no business in your house. And I have no intention of being your mistress."

"Then—then what will you do? Where will you go?"

"That is no concern of yours. You must think of yourself, and your best course will be to do as I have advised you. Be married."

He looked at her speechlessly, and as he did so Harriet was overcome by a such a wave of tenderness that she nearly took him in her arms. But she drew back, an expression of resolve coming onto her face. Turning on her heel, she went to the door.

"In any event, your problems are hardly my concern any longer," she said.

The next moment she was gone.

Long after this, Richard was at last able to sob himself to sleep in such a passion of misery and desolation as he had never known.

CHAPTER FIVE

All the next day Richard existed in a kind of gloomy torpor. At once fatigued and restless, he could fix his attention on nothing, and was at last reduced to gazing through the library window, that same window composed of colored lozenges of glass whose different hues had varied the view of the street four long years ago, when he had been awaiting Harriet's return after their first interview.

Now, as on that day, it was raining. For an instant he had a curious impression of time have turned backwards, of that first period of waiting being repeated. It was as if nothing at all had happened since then and he was back where he had started from, with all the beauty, excitement and suffering of the last five years to be experienced once again. With a sigh of misery, he drew away from the window and passed into the hall. He put on his mackintosh and let himself out into the wet street. He felt the need for exercise, if only as a distraction from his loneliness.

The fine rain was still falling, and the wet pavements gleamed with the reflection of the gaslamps. The street was empty, but from nearby, from the maze of streets to the east, came a steady discordant hum, a medley of indistinguishable sounds betokening human life and movement. He had walked a hundred yards along Great Portland Street before he was aware of these noises of the unknown quarter little more than a block away. Moving instinctively, he turned down the first street towards them, and in five minutes found himself plunged in the midst of one the most raucous, slatternly districts of London.

Facing the glare of the gin palace at the corner of Marleybone and Charlton Streets, he paused uncertainly before this revelation of the city—the uncouth squalor of the straight narrow streets with their tall flat-faced terraces of dingy three-storied houses, their broken steps and crazy railing, their garbage-littered gutters.

Through the closed window-sashes, whoops of drunken laughter could be heard, and the brutish alternation of strident quarrelling and stupefied debauch. Almost every doorway stood open the lights from the passages showing in silhouette the cloaked figures of women standing on the threshold. As men strolled past the doors they were followed by low calls, whistles, and the sound of rapping on window-panes. Here and there, in some dark alley framing her outline against a dim light, a woman would lift her skirts, briefly displaying to the passer-by the smooth-shaven vulva of prostitution.

The boy walked on blindly, looking straight in front of him. Through his brain a single thought

was running monotonously: She is leaving me forever, in a week. In a week, forever...

The streets grew quieter, and the houses took on
an appearance of greater respectability, as he
approached the district that catered to the most ele-
gant and decorous forms of vice. This was the
region of the well-decorated rooms, of the costlier
bagnios, the houses of assignation, the establish-
ments of the masseuses. The boy saw nothing.
When a woman stepped from an archway and took
him gently by the arm, he stopped and looked at
her blankly.

She was not young, but her face was handsome.
A pair of soft eyes, rendered larger by the pen-
cilling on their lids and edges, glowed in the darkness. Her tall ample form was wrapped in a rich
cloak, her head bare. Her voice reached him, with a
low French accent. The tenderness of its tone
pierced through the fog of misery in which his senses were obscured.

"Poor boy," she said simply. "Poor boy, what are
you doing here?"

He did not reply, but made no movement to dis-
engage himself. His face felt stiff and frozen, but he
felt his lips beginning to tremble as if of themselves.

The woman looked at him more intently, taking
in the youth and beauty of his white, miserable
face. She reached for his hand. "So young, and so
unhappy!" she said. "That is not right. Come with
me..."

Moving as if in a trance, he let her lead him
under the archway, then along a dark passage to a
door which she opened. He paused, but the pressure on his arm was gentle and insistent. He went
in.

The room was small, warm, and bathed in a dim,

luminous glow of rose. In the semi-darkness, nothing could be seen but a great cushioned armchair on which a doll sat with its legs apart, a high bench placed against the wall, and a wide, low divan. There was a faint odor of musk in the air. The boy let his companion remove his cap and coat, and submitted to the strong, soft pull of her arms as she drew him to the couch. They sank down side by side, her body enfolding his in a tender, protective movement to which he yielded with a sensation of weariness and resignation.

"Poor boy," she murmured again. "Tell me what it is, my dear."

His grief suddenly welled up in him. Without a word he buried his head in her breasts and burst into tears.

"Yes, yes..." the French voice continued. "That is better, that is much better." Her hand stroked his hair with a firm yet delicate touch.

His tears flowed faster. As they did so his sobbing gradually subsided, his breathing lengthened, attuning itself more and more to the gentle, regular swell with which the woman's own breasts rose and fell beneath his cheeks. The sharpness of his grief had now almost disappeared, giving place to a vague sadness that he indulged with an almost voluptuous sense of relief. He became aware of the woman.

She had removed her cloak, and he felt the lustrous, smoothly stretched satin that encased her body; opening his eyes, he saw the contours against which his own flesh was pressed—the narrow waist, the great haunches, the jut of the swelling breast. It was imprisoned so tightly in the shimmering black bodice that the nipples stood out with a frank unabashed splendor. Instinctively, his hand reached out to this magnificent bosom.

She laughed softly. "That is right, my dear," she said. "Feel my breasts. It will help you. Have no fear, they are for you. Ah, you like them, do you not? You like my good breasts, you little rogue?"

He murmured indistinctly, his hands curving around her bosom. His throat had become dry, his eyes were fixed on the two shining points that centered this superb chest.

"Yes," he heard her whisper, "they please you, that is good. You wish to kiss them now? Come then, kiss them as you desire. They are yours. There, see—" Her hand went to the high neck of her bodice. In an instant her bosom was stripped bare, its treasures spread out before him.

He gave a gasp of pleasure, his hands grasped for the hard white swelling flesh. He felt her clasp his head, bringing his mouth to one of the firm rosy points. As his lips closed on it, he was swept by such a wave of ecstasy that his whole body grew weak, his head spun deliciously, and he lost consciousness.

Richard came to himself slowly, luxuriously, the rose light of the little room stealing under his eyelids. It was like waking from a happy dream. He became aware that he was lying on the couch, quite nude, with the woman's arm was around his neck. He saw that she had fastened her bodice again. She was looking at him with an air of pleasure mingled with reproof.

"Foolish boy," she said. "You must not love a woman's body like that. It is not good to be so passionate. You will harm yourself so. Rest now, you must rest for a few minutes."

Hardly hearing what she said, he sighed happily.

His hand reached for her breasts again. "Please—oh, please," he murmured, "let me see...again—"

She caught his fingers. "No," she said softly. "You have seen enough. You are still too nervous. You will soon be better. Rest now. I will give you some pleasure later."

He relaxed against her, a deep, ineffable peace stealing over him, a state of mind in which he was able for a while to forget all the misery of the past month, the loneliness, the racking and unassuaged desire, the prospect of losing the woman he loved. As if part of the woman into the hallow of whose superb body he lay pressed, feeling himself drifting before the strong regular swell of her breath to which his own was timed once more, as if blown over the sea of darkness that appeared to his lulled senses as rocking like an enormous cradle, he lay like a tiny island of drugged consciousness, locked in the woman's embrace.

"Are you better now?" she asked, stroking his cheek, on which the tears were already dry. "Yes...Now, I will put the strength back into you. Come, lie down, and I will rub you. It is what you need."

He let her take him to the high padded bench, and stretched himself out obediently, face down, abandoning himself to her entirely. Her hands gripped him firmly for an instant, and then began kneading the muscles of his neck with strong, practised fingers. He sighed deeply, feeling the physical tension of his body slackening. It was as if all the strain and weariness of his limbs were being dissolved and drawn out by these cunning hands, which seemed to understand the very structure of his being. She passed to his shoulders, then to his

173

feet, his legs, his thighs. He began to feel refreshed, calmed, invigorated. Her fingers kneaded his loins.

"You have a beautiful body," she said.

He opened his eyes wide, a thrill of pleasure passing through him at her words. He had never thought of his body.

"It is not very strong," he murmured, flushing.

She ground her knuckles, firmly, skillfully, into the bones of his spine, one by one.

"Beauty is more than strength," she said. It sounded, he thought, like a quotation.

Then he felt the pressure of her hands changing as they passed up and down over his skin, lingering over it. Her touch became lighter. Her fingers felt like flower petals now, as they made slow circles on his shoulders, ran down his back and over his loins, then looped and crossed and curled deftly up in the tender hollows of his sides like a wave licking the shore. The caress was repeated, with reversals, additions, variations, like some beautiful complicated arabesque.

"Oh," he murmured with a shiver. "That is nice…"

She laughed softly. Her fingers passed lightly between his thighs, brushing the anus, bringing him sensations still more exquisite.

"Yes," she said, "it is nice…very nice, is it not?" Her hands continued to busy themselves, exploring the region of his testicles with consummate skill. They paused in their task. "Now turn over, please."

All at once he realized that his penis was standing stiffly, and was stricken with dismay. He did not move.

"If you please," she said gravely. Her palm

174

smacked his thigh lightly, authoritatively.

He gasped with embarrassment. Then he rolled over on the bench, closing his eyes tightly. "I—I…" he stammered.

"Hush…"

She continued passing her fingers over him lightly, covering him with the tracery of the same delicate, maddening caress. As if by accident, the soft underside of her wrist brushed the taut underside of his straining member lightly, almost furtively, at the end of an upward stroke. He throbbed and shivered involuntarily. Again her hand brushed him. His eyes were fixed on her in a mute, tremulous appeal.

But it was not the smiling painted face and high pompadour of the masseuse he saw above him now. It was the austere, beautiful countenance of Harriet Marwood that swam before his eyes. The beloved features of the governess were recalled to him so vividly in this moment that he grew suddenly dizzy, sick with a sense of the unfaithfulness comprised in his acquiescence in this special caress. For at this point she had begun to stroke his member softly, directly, maddening his senses.

"Oh…please, no!" he cried. "Not that, please!"

The woman stopped and regarded him. "No?" she said, a little smile curving her lips. "You do not like that, my dear?" She paused, shaking her head reprovingly. "You wish to go to bed with me then? Is that your desire, little rogue?"

He did not understand her meaning. But now, sitting up, he caught sight of the open door leading to a further room, where in the deeper darkness a wide bed could be seen. "Yes, yes," he whispered, seizing on her words. "Take me to bed with you. That is all I want, please—nothing but that."

"Nothing but that, indeed! What a young man it is! Tell me now, how old are you?"

He looked at her uncomprehendingly. "Twenty-one," he lied.

"Is that true?" She looked in his face carefully. "I would have thought you much younger. Yes, you are not too young to have a woman..." She laughed. "Come now, my little virgin, and I will make a man of you for nothing."

The next moment he was lying in the cool, perfumed bed, watching her as with slow, accustomed movements she stripped off her gown. In a minute she stood beside him, nude save for her long black silk stockings. With arms raised and hands locked behind her head turned slowly around so that he could see every angle of her statuesque body—the glorious fall of the reins, the great hips, and the swelling mound of Venus between her thighs. When she stepped gracefully into the bed and laid her body against his, he gave a cry and pulled her to him in a frenzy desire.

"Ah," she smiled. "You are in a hurry. Let it be so, then." And rolling on her strong back, she opened her thighs and drew him on top of her with a practiced motion. Her hands lightly caressed his genitals for an instant, then guided his erect member between the velvet lips of her warm vulva which already began to move and to clasp it deliciously as the masseuse rotated her hips with insinuating skill.

"That is good," she said softly. "You are learning to fuck now, aren't you? Yes, it comes easily to you. You fuck very well. You will please a woman."

She parted his buttocks, and her finger found his anus and entered it softly. "Now ride me to your pleasure, dear little virgin..." Her silken legs crept up and locked around his waist, her loins cradling him with a soft rocking motion.

His breath came faster, he began to leap and plunge, driving his member deeply into the hot clinging sheath of this delicious womb, which kept rolling and twisting expertly, kneading and massaging the head of his penis with the firm, persistent action of the vaginal muscles.

But his eyes were tightly closed. It was not the masseuse he was possessing, he kept telling himself frantically, it was Harriet herself, it had to be her. "Oh Harriet, Harriet," he kept murmuring under his breath, and was only answered by sighs and soft professional obscenities.

Gradually his movements slowed and flagged, his penis began to yield. In vain he redoubled the stroke of his hips, rocking and thrusting in desperation. It was no use. His erection was leaving him, the sperm was withdrawing deep within him again. And suddenly overcome by fear and self-loathing he broke free of her hold and stood up.

"I—I cannot..." he stammered. "I must go."

"Poor boy," she murmured, rising also. "Yes, you had better go."

He dressed hurriedly, his fingers trembling, his knees weak. "I could not—" he began. The words would still not come.

"Say nothing. Come, let me kiss you now, and we will say goodbye." She bent over and kissed him tenderly on the forehead. Then she opened the door. "Go now. Go back to your love, whomever she may be."

He found himself again in the wet, cold street, conscious only of his escape from a consummation that would have stood for an act of supreme infidelity.

As he wandered back through the streets it began to rain heavily. The downpour beat on his head and shoulders with the effect of an icy shower-bath. Instinctively, he opened his clothing and let the rain pour over him, seeking to wash himself clean of the vile contact he had undergone, of the traces of those hideous caresses that had fired his flesh, to sluice away the memory of that soilure in the perfumed bed.

All at once he stopped and raised his face to the black, teeming sky. "Dear God," he said in a calm, intense voice, "if I am not yet utterly soiled, if I was saved by my inability to possess that woman, then witness my vow to make amends to Harriet.

CHAPTER SIX

In the meantime, Mr. Lovel and Kate had been tasting the most unalloyed happiness they had ever known. After briefly sojourning in all the capitals of Europe, and sampling the delights of the most luxurious brothels in Paris, Berlin, Vienna, Rome and Constantinople, they had at last settled in an enchanting region of the Mediterranean coast, where Mr. Lovel had bought a small but magnificent villa on a beautiful point on the ocean. And here they began to put into practice the various ideas suggested to them by their insatiable lubricity.

For some time now they had been invoking the assistance of youth to grace their ruttish exercises. The practice had been begun in a Paris brothel by accident, where they both had taken a fancy to a young, pretty black girl who was an inmate there. Her good nature and special skill in sucking the anus and testicles had first roused their interest in her. Kate, although no lesbian, declared she had never had her arsehole so well tongued in her life, while Arthur himself experienced the delightful novelty of having the girl take his testicles in her warm pink mouth and massage them with her tongue at her same time as Kate herself was sucking his member.

These circumstances had led to their taking the talented black girl into their travelling entourage, where she served them as both maid and assistant to their pleasures. By the time they settled in the Mediterranean villa their household had been further augmented by a young Turkish boy whose passionate and exclusive addiction of sucking vulvas endeared him to Kate, and in whose hot elastic rectum Mr. Lovel often took a turn by way of variety. A statuesque middle-aged German woman named Lottchen, a former masseuse whose superb and enormous breasts, combined with her boundless experience in all the most perverse and licentious sexual practices, was also a member of the household. She was well fitted her for various ancillary roles in the grand task of heightening and reanimating Mr. Lovel's rabid sensuality. Moreover, these two individuals performed the additional functions of gardener and housekeeper.

And so, a few days after the tender scene we have just described between Richard and Harriet Marwood, this fortunate couple were disposed in the cool private garden of the Mediterranean property. Arthur, reclining in a long chair, was allowing himself to be gently stirred by the sight of Kate being slowly and expertly sucked by the naked Turkish boy. The light sighs and little moans of pleasure his mistress emitted from time to time afforded him, as usual, a tranquil and serene joy.

"Why, my dear Kate," he said after a while, "Is not Ali giving you some special pleasure this evening? You seem more deeply stirred than usual. Have you taught him some new tricks with his tongue, by any chance?"

"Oh no, Arthur," said Kate, "The dear child needs no teaching. He is just a little more passionate this evening. Look at his little prick, see how it stands up! We must have Lottchen frig him soon, I think. Would you like that, little boy? No, no, do not answer me!" she said. "Do not dare stop now.

"Ah, that is good, Arthur," she continued. "He sucks divinely, with such delicacy that there is no strain at all. Indeed, I shall never finish saying how grateful I am to you for affording me this boy, my heart's darling." She smiled mistily at her protector over the boy's dark curly head as she pressed it between her parted thighs. "I'm thinking, Arthur, that you are the kindest and dearest lover ever a woman had."

"Why, Kate, it is half selfishness, for your pleasure wakens mine, you know. See," and he drew aside his silk robe and displayed his already firming member. "That is as much Ali's work as is the moisture in your own vulva at this moment."

Kate surveyed the beloved shaft with delight. "Ah, you must put it into me soon, Arthur! For all I like the boy's tongue tickling and playing in my cunt, there's nothing like the thrust of a good hard prick to make a woman spend the way she should, and yours is the best and hardest in the world for me.

"But there is Louise with your drink," she said as the nude black woman came from the house carrying a tray.

Arthur's hands caressed the girl's dusky buttocks, his fingers swiftly finding the rosy and wrinkled aperture of Sodom and tickling it shrewdly as she set the tinkling tumbler at his elbow. At this signal, even before he had time to speak, the pretty woman dropped to her knees and took his penis into her wide-lipped mouth.

"By heaven, Kate," he said after a few moments, "the girl is really learning how to milk a man's member!"

Kate laughed. "And Louise, are you not forgetting what I told you, my girl, that you should use your tongue and lips together if you're to give a man the real pleasure. Do not leave your hands idle either, but squeeze his balls thus. That is what a man likes when you're sucking him—is it not, Arthur?"

But at this moment there was a sudden interruption. Before Mr. Lovel could reply to his mistress' question, the portly figure of the German masseuse appeared. She too was naked. This absence of costume was almost required in the Lovel household. The woman surveyed the lubricious scene before her for a moment with gleaming eyes, then recollected her errand and handed Mr. Lovel the telegram.

He tore it open, and at once slapped his thigh in delight. "Ah listen to this, Kate—here's marvellous news: 'HARRIET AND I BEING MARRIED TODAY. WISH ME JOY. RICHARD.' Why, this is the best news I could have!"

Kate clapped her hands. "Now isn't that a grand thing!"

Arthur was literally beaming from ear to ear. "By God, Kate, there goes the last of my worries. The boy is in the best hands at last. That young woman will manage his money and him both, and she has more brains than most. What great luck!"

"Ah, and they are both lucky too, I think. For they are well suited."

"I should hope so," said Mr. Lovel. "That girl can do anything she sets her mind to. Come now, this calls for a celebration." He rose, drawing the bulb of his now fully erected member from the woman's warm and salivating mouth, and caressed it himself for a moment, beaming at the naked members of his household as they stood around him. "Louise my dear, serve that magnum of champagne that's been chilling so long. We must all drink a toast to my son and his bride."

In a few minutes they were drinking, their glassed raised in repeated toasts to the young couple in faraway London, pledging to their long life, happiness and pleasure in the state of wedlock.

"And now," said Mr. Lovel, when they were all gaily stimulated, "we shall continue our celebration. And as the bearer of this good news needs some special reward, you shall help me to spend between Lottchen's breasts."

He knelt on the long chair, and at once they look their places—the masseuse lying with her chest between his legs, the black woman taking his testicles in her mouth from beneath, and Ali spreading his employer's buttocks for the insertion of his active tongue. Mr. Lovel then laid his glowing prick between Lottchen's superb breasts, which she pressed together on each side so as to embed it completely in the warm and snowy crease, and then began to masturbate him with the soft friction of the great swelling globes.

Mr. Lovel's eyes gleamed with pleasure as he thus felt the whole region of his loins flooded by delicious sensation. "Kate, Kate," he cried, "come and tickle yourself in front of me! For it wants only that to complete my happiness."

But his mistress was already standing above him with parted legs, her moist genitals a few inches from his face. "Oh, Arthur," she said, "that is what I don't need to be told to do. The sight of you taking your pleasure in that fine way is a sight to start any woman to frigging herself." And she began titillating the ruby point of her clitoris before his enraptured eyes.

In this situation, we must leave Arthur Lovel. And in fact we may well believe that is how he would best like to be left—in a state of voluptuous ecstasy and with every genital sense being entertained. His anus and testicles are being expertly titillated by a pair of avid mouths, the throbbing head of his member is sliding in the satiny trough of a pair of large and snowy breasts, and his adored mistress is joyfully masturbating herself before his eyes.

CHAPTER SEVEN

At this very moment Harriet and Richard had just returned in a cab from the registry office where the clerical dexterity of a magistrate had made them one.

The youth was in a fever of impatience to assert his marital rights: whenever he turned his eyes on the tall young woman who had so recently been his governess and who was now his wife, his gaze lit up with desire and his breath came with shorter respiration.

Now, for almost the first time that day, he noticed her appearance and was aware of her clothes—the tight jacket edged with fur, the frilled and scalloped skirt, and the bonnet which was no more than a bandeau of fur and velvet tied round her high, tilted chignon. Now, too, he noticed the startling increase in her beauty during the last year.

Indeed, Harriet was a strikingly beautiful

woman. Though she still held her tall figure very erect, all angularity and stiffness had disappeared from her carriage, just as the lines of her mouth had become fuller and softer without losing any of their air of firmness and decision. Her face, older now and more rounded in its contours, had the increased charm of maturity. The glance of the violet-grey eyes was characterized less by the stern energy of her girlhood than by a certain quiet confidence. Her assurance was so marked as to give the expression of her whole face a certain voluptuous placidity. It was as if to suggest that this assurance was allied with the rich and thoughtful sensuality lurking just behind her eyes.

Oh, the youth was thinking, to believe that I am about to possess this magnificent creature—soon, soon—this very night!

But Harriet had her own plans for their first married encounter. After dinner she rose and fixed him with her great grey eyes.

"I am going to retire now, Richard," she said. "You will not help me to undress tonight. You will simply come to my room at ten o'clock. Do you understand?"

He had already risen before she began speaking. His disappointment was all too evident. But, long broken to the habit of unquestioning obedience, he dropped his eyes with a murmur of assent.

At the appointed hour, naked under his dressing gown, he tapped at her door and was bidden to enter. The curtains were drawn, the room was bathed in the subdued light of a single shaded lamp, and Harriet, in a loose white negligée, was seated in a large armchair beside the fire. He paused, dazzled by the breathtaking loveliness of her face. His untutored glance could not tell that

Harriet had, for this occasion, made use of certain
artificial aids to beauty.

She remained silent under his gaze, keeping her
own eyes fixed on the fire with an air of dreamy
absorption, letting the flickering firelight cast its
glistening reflection under her long eyelashes.
When she spoke at last, still not looking at him, it
was in a low thoughtful voice.

"This is our wedding night, my dear, and I hope
you are thoroughly imbued with the sense of its
solemnity for both of us in the years to come.
Richard, you may have some preconceived ideas
of the roles of man and wife, ideas influenced by
the generally held view that it is the man who is
instigator and leader in the tender relations that
must subsist between them. If you have any such
ideas, you may put them out of your head immediately."

She paused, and turned her calm gaze on him
for first time. "For you must realize that in this
marriage it is I who will rule, and you who will
obey—above all in the matter of our most intimate
connections. Do you understand?"

Still only half grasping the import of her words,
he lowered his eyes. "Yes, Harriet," he murmured.

"Good. You must also realize that it is my sensations and my wishes that will take precedence at
all times. It will be your concern, above everything
else, to give me pleasure. Your own pleasure is of
quite secondary importance. I understand that to
bring this home to you I shall have to instruct you
in your proper behavior towards me, for you know
absolutely nothing of woman's needs and desires.
Perhaps you think that the possession and employment of a male organ is all that is required to
make you a suitable partner for a passionate

woman like myself. If you do so, you are wrong."

She paused, uncrossed her legs slowly and parted her thighs. "You have never yet seen my genitals, Richard, and I believe that your course of instruction had best begin by your doing so." She paused once again, taking the edges of her robe in either hand. "Go down on your knees, Richard." He obeyed breathlessly. Harriet lifted the white robe above her waist. There was a short silence.

Richard gazed at a vulva of surpassing beauty. A pair of small lips surmounted by a clitoris of unusual prominence and surrounded by fine curly hair as black as night. Deliberately, Harriet parted the lips with her fingers, disclosing the moist pink flesh of the interior. When she spoke her voice was low and compelling.

"Look well, Richard. For this will be for you, from now on, not the source or avenue of your pleasure, not the sign even of my sex and the index of my sensuality, but something much more. It will be for you, from now on and for always, an object of adoration. Your sole concern will be to minister to it in every way. It does not matter that at present you know nothing of those ways. Just as I have taught you many things in the past when I was your governess, I will teach you the ways in which you must please me now that I am your wife. Do you follow me?"

His throat was dry. He could not speak, but merely nodded. His eyes were fixed between her thighs, as if they could never leave this region wherein his whole desire and worship were now concentrated. He heard Harriet speaking as if in a dream.

"There are other areas of sensation in my body to whose pleasure you will also be expected to contribute," she said quietly, "but you will learn about them, and what each requires, later on. This evening you will begin by bringing me satisfaction in this very center of my desires…"

She lifted her body slightly, raising and placing her thighs on either of the wide padded arms of the chair she sat in, bringing the beautiful clitoris into still greater prominence.

"Bring your head between my knees now," she said. "And now open your lips and kiss me there with your whole mouth. That is all I require of you at this time."

As he brought his lips to the exquisite cleft, he received an intoxicating odor that seemed to breathe from it. Almost fainting with rapture, he pressed his mouth to it and then, actuated by some instinct or atavistic intelligence, darted his tongue deeply within the warm and musky confines. He received at the same time the message of her aroused senses, and the light pressure of her hand on his head as if in conscious recognition of his impromptu caress.

"Yes, my dear," she murmured. "Now take my clitoris between your lips and suck it firmly." And she sank back luxuriously in her chair.

For the next minutes, under her laconic directions, Richard licked and sucked and kissed the superb vulva with greedy enjoyment. Never, he thought, had he tasted such bliss as in the performance of this sensual exercise for the pleasure of the woman he idolized. He drank in the sound of her sighs and moans, feasted on the massage conveyed by the undulations of her hips, the shuddering of her ventral muscles and the very twitching of the responsive organ itself. He slid between her legs, throbbing with the tension of desire and his craving to ejaculate. But it was only when Harriet reached her crisis, and clasping his head tightly between her quivering thighs, discharged over his face and mouth, that he realized that she was on this occasion quite careless of any pleasure but her own.

Her praise and gratitude for his efforts made him some amends. But he was stricken with dismay when a few minutes later, again parting her thighs, she made him resume his efforts.

This time she was even more exigent. In tones of increasing urgency, she ordered him to redouble the speed and penetration of his caresses. When with the muscles of his tongue became numb with fatigue, he felt himself at last unable to respond, she suddenly exploded with wrath.

"Wretched boy," she said, suddenly drawing herself up. "You did not think I meant what I said earlier, did you? I see there is still only one way for you to learn..." And picking up the whip she lashed his back and sides savagely. "Now, down with your head and finish my pleasure properly!"

He gasped with pain. Then, calling on all the resources of his strength, he buried his face between her thighs and brought her to orgasm again.

Twice more that night he was obliged to repeat this service before she was satisfied. By this time, his tongue was painful and swollen, his lips were smarting from the repeated strokes of the whip, and the unsatisfied desire of his own body was swallowed up in the aching fatigue of every nerve in his loins.

Harriet, her body once more covered, looked at him with a faint smile. "You see, Richard," she said, "that the duties of a husband are not all they are popularly represented to be. In your case, indeed, they have so far brought you more pain than pleasure. Come here now and tell me: you are a little disappointed, are you not?"

As she had done so often in the past, she drew him between her knees, placed her hands between his legs and stroked his pendent member.

He tried to smile, then suddenly put his hands to his face and burst into tears.

"Come now," laughed Harriet. "You are not a very gallant bridegroom at the moment. Let me see if I cannot restore you at least to a more manly appearance."

In spite of his shame, misery, and fatigue, his penis was soon standing stiffly under her skillful hands.

"See," she said, "now you look a little better. You are feeling a little better too, is it not so?"

His only answer was to throw himself into her arms in passion of reawakened desire. His hips began to thrust blindly against her body.

She laughed again. "Well, Richard, what does this mean?"

"Harriet, Harriet," he cried, "please do not be so cruel. Now that we are married, am I not—are you not going to—to let me—" He was unable to finish, and with one hand he gestured miserably towards his straining member.

"To let you put it into me?" she said dryly. "Why, no, Richard. We are not ready for that yet."

"N-not ready? But I don't understand! I thought—I thought..."

"You thought you were going to enjoy me and spend in me, did you not? Well, Richard, that is out of the question at the moment."

He looked at her in numb bewilderment.

She suddenly became serious. "Listen to me, Richard. Listen very carefully. You know," she said in a low voice, "there is one aspect of our marriage that I have never discussed with you. It is a matter on which modesty might well oblige me to keep silent, but which, I believe, should be properly aired before we go any further."

"Yes, Harriet," he murmured.

"It is the question of children."

He looked up at her in dismay, and was about to speak when she checked him.

"I must tell you, my dear, that we shall have no children. I do not wish it."

His heart leapt up joyfully. "Why, Harriet—of—of course not. I had never thought of it, and—and really, I do not wish for children either. It shall be as you say."

She smiled with genuine amusement at his declaration. "I am glad to hear you say so, my boy. But to ensure there shall be none, we must take proper measures, you know."

He laid his head on her knees. "I—I know nothing of these matters, Harriet. But I am willing to do whatever you say…"

Her voice continued quietly. "Thank you, my dear. I will tell you what is. You must submit to a trifling piece of surgery before I can be entirely yours. That is all."

He looked up, his face suddenly transfigured. "And that is all? Then—then you will make—make me happy after all? You will—give yourself to me once this is done?"

"Yes, Richard," she said quietly.

"Then let it be soon—soon!" he cried. "For I cannot wait…"

She leaned over and embraced him tenderly.

"Dear Richard," she said, "I also am impatient to give myself to you."

The words, combined with the renewed pressure of her hand between his thighs, made his penis stand once again.

"Then, Harriet," he murmured, "will you not—not play with me tonight? I need it—oh so badly..."

"Masturbate you?" she said coolly. "Why no, my dear, I think not. It will be better for you to possess yourself in patience until you are in the condition where I can be safely and entirely yours. It will not be long. Now kiss me goodnight and go to your room. And be sure you behave yourself."

"Oh Harriet," he murmured, as he raised his lips from hers, "You know you have cured me of that habit long ago, that I simply cannot give myself pleasure any more."

She laughed. "And is not that as it should be? Are you not glad of a circumstance that makes you entirely mine in thought and deed?"

CHAPTER EIGHT

The following day, after the surgeon left, Harriet remained at Richard's side to nurse him through the few hours required for his recovery. It was she who, with infinite gentleness, changed the dressing on his tiny wound, and restrained him from rising from bed that day. For, once his initial terror had passed, his trepidation gave place to such liveliness and high spirits that he was almost unmanageable. Seeing the last bar to their union removed, he was inwardly wild with impatience to bury his penis in the vulva of whose passionate responsiveness he was already so well assured from the events of the wedding night. In vain did Harriet try to persuade him to sleep.

"Oh Harriet," he exclaimed for the twentieth time, "I am so happy, so excited, that I am sure I could not."

Seated beside his bed, she surveyed him calmly. "But you must rest, my dear. Tomorrow will be quite time enough for you to get up."

"Tomorrow?" His face fell. "Then I am not to—we will not sleep together tonight?"

Her face softened, "No, my dear. Do you desire it so greatly? Already?"

He did not reply, but her hand beneath the bed-clothes was already verifying the state of his passion. At this moment the temptation to test his sexual reactions after the operation was irresistible, and suddenly drawing aside the covers she bent down and took his penis in her mouth.

He observed the action with astonishment. Never had he imagined the possibility of such a caress, and it struck both his imagination and his senses with all the force of the maddest and most voluptuous novelty. The moist heat of her mouth and the action of her tongue against the tender underside of his member, together with the almost incredible fact that it was the feared and idolized Harriet herself who was gratifying him in this unheard-of manner, made him almost lose his senses in ecstasy. When his sperm at last jetted in her throat, it was released with an intensity he had never known before.

"There now, Richard," she murmured, patting his subsiding penis softly, "That was pleasant, was it not?"

His only answer was to throw his arms about her neck in a passion of tenderness. He was penetrated as much by overwhelming gratitude as by the sheer beauty of an experience so fraught with delight that he could barely believe in it.

Harriet stroked the yellow curls of the handsome young head pressed in the hollow of her neck. The boundless affection of his nature suddenly touched her to depths of tenderness she had never suspected in herself. She passed her fingers softly over his cheek.

"Ah, Richard," she said. "You are only beginning to realize what a delightful institution marriage can be, or all the pleasures open to man and wife."

He tightened his embrace. "Then," he whispered, "you will do this to me again?"

She smiled against his cheek. "I shall do it to you constantly, Richard. Yes, and many other things of which you as yet know nothing, but which I shall show you."

"Oh, Harriet," he breathed, "then there are still other pleasures to come from you?"

"Yes, my dear, many others. But of them all, there is none better than the act of full possession, as you will find once your member is within me."

They remained motionless, locked in each other's arms. When Harriet spoke again her voice was trembling slightly.

"And now, my dear, that you have resigned your last male prerogative, now that you can never beget a child and no rival can ever come between us, now that you are the instrument of my endless pleasure and nothing more, now I can love you as I desire and as you deserve. Never think I will forget this sacrifice you have made for me, my dear." She paused, and tightened her embrace still more to conceal the fact that she herself was close to tears. "It will not be long now, Richard. And believe me, I am as impatient to be yours as you are to make me so."

"Oh, but when, Harriet?" he whispered. "When?"

She recovered herself, and smiled. "Why, I am at heart a woman of sentiment, you know," she said with a lightness by which she sought to cover the depth of her emotion. "When you possess me, I wish it to be in the surroundings where I first learned to love you—in the house at Christchurch. Yes, Richard, that is where we shall spend our honeymoon."

EPILOGUE

We are aware that is not customary to pursue the fortunes of the characters in a romance once they are married, in deference, possibly, to the notion that nothing that can be said of their life could do justice to its almost super-mundane bliss, and because there is little in their behavior whose description would not violate the most elementary laws of propriety. That we have, however, so far dared to follow our hero and heroine past the sacred portals of matrimony, is due solely to the special exigencies of our story itself, which require that its climax be demonstrated in accordance with what has gone before.

The only omission we are obliged to make is one that is enforced on us by the usual limitations of our ability, for the ecstasy in which Richard literally swam when he at last plunged his fine nervous member into Harriet's vulva is something that our poor pen cannot describe. We must be content to indicate the excess of his sensations by saying that his first orgasm in the womb of his beloved was so violent that he fainted quite away.

The honeymoon was passed, as Harriet had planned, in the absolute seclusion of the house at Christchurch, in the same surroundings which she had found so well adapted to the strict training of the boy only four years earlier. The same domestic arrangements were made for the comfort and privacy of the young couple. Only the timetable of the days was altered in the interests of later rising and earlier retiring. Thus the regular routine and the sequestered life that had so favoured the application of the severest discipline by the governess were recalled and recreated to serve the softer but no less rigorous demands of the wife.

For two weeks, the house in the woods was a veritable abode of love. Its walls, which had once echoed so often to puerile screams and the insistent whistle of cane and martinet, were now filled at all hours of the day and night with soft murmurs and the sound of kisses, with deep-drawn breaths and low continuous cries.

During this period, Richard was inducted into all the mysteries of voluptuousness. He learned what it was to be caressed from head to foot with the most consummate skill, and to have not only his member but his anus sucked to the limits of their capacity for sensation. Moreover, Harriet's whole body came to engross his attention, calling him to its center as to an irreducible absolute, so that the whole region of her loins became for him not only the center and focus of his desire but an area of genuine worship. He was never happier than when lying for hours together between her thighs, his mouth glued to her vulva. Its need and every sensual vagary his tongue now understood and took delight in satisfying. In short, Harriet had made of him a finished libertine, a connoisseur of every kind of delight to be enjoyed with a woman.

For her part, she continued to exult in the possession of a youth who was not only made to receive pleasure but to bestow it. She found that his appetite for her body was almost insatiable: the slightest touch of her hand, even the glance of her eye, was enough to provoke him to immediate erection, and once his member was sheathed in her vulva she found its vigor and persistence all that she could have hoped for. Richard, indeed, otherwise so passive and weak-willed, assumed another character in bed. One would have said he was made for nothing else but to gratify a woman's lusts, that this was his single and supreme mission in life.

She was well aware, however, that it was she who had made him so. With her deep knowledge of his nature, she was waiting for this idyllic period of their relations to come to an end, and for the results of her long and severe training to be justified.

It was autumn before the hour of proof arrived.

That day it had rained all afternoon, with a warm persistent drizzle that discouraged any activity out of doors and left the young couple to their own devices. Harriet, not displeased by the circumstances, had carried her beloved youth to bed as soon as luncheon was over. In the great bedroom, which had once been hers alone and which was now the arena of their loves, the happy pair had passed the entire afternoon, exchanging embraces—each more leisurely, passionate and prolonged than the last. They sunk at last into a condition of blissful exhaustion from which they were roused only by Molly's discreet summons to dinner.

This was no unusual programme for the lovers, and had heretofore been followed by the chastest of good nights and a long restorative slumber. But this evening Harriet, whose desires were accustomed to increase with the waning year, was still unsated. When she rejoined her husband in bed that evening it was to clasp him once more in her arms, with a fresh and importunate desire that the enervated youth was unable to return.

His limbs drooping with fatigue, his eyelids heavy with sleep, he was unable to rouse himself. Harriet redoubled her efforts, striving to reanimate him by the caresses of her hands and her breasts. In vain did she stroke and flatter the whole region of his loins. In vain did she display her moist and throbbing vulva before his eyes. In vain did she take his flaccid member in her mouth and seek to revive it by the most vigorous suction. It was no use, and she was left pressed against his sleeping body in a fever of unappeased desire.

Richard was indeed quite worn out. He slept heavily, dreamlessly, his whole body relaxed and quiescent. How long he had slept he did not know, but he was borne back reluctantly into wakefulness by a sensation of coldness coupled with the sound of Harriet's voice. He opened his eyes, and for a few moments he did not know where he was. He believed he was a child again, lying naked on his bed and shuddering before the most familiar and dreaded vision of his boyhood.

Harriet was standing at the bedside. She wore the long hooded cape, her face set in lines of extraordinary severity, and the black riding-whip quivered in her hand. Her voice was cold and clear.

"Come, Richard, it is time. Get up at once."

He stared at her, once more a terror-stricken boy anticipating the bite of the lash on his buttocks. Then, still as if he were in the clutches of a nightmare, he rolled out of bed, found his feet and bent over submissively. From behind him he heard the brisk premonitory whistling of the whip as it cut the air, and heard his governess—ah, it was not his wife now, it was his governess!—addressing him in the room he knew so well.

"You know, Richard, why you are to be flogged, do you not?"

The voice paused, and the lash touched his shrinking flesh lightly. "Listen: I must remind you that your status as husband involves certain duties, and that when we were married you assumed the responsibility of performing them at all times. At all times, you understand! Until this evening you have behaved yourself well, but a few hours ago you refused to gratify me."

The whip touched him again. "When I was your governess, you knew the result of any act of disobedience. Now that I am your wife, you will find that my methods have not changed. You are going to be whipped now, Richard, until you decide to satisfy me. Do you understand?"

"Yes, Harriet..." He was still only half awake, and his feelings were in a turmoil.

"Good," she continued. "You are not to think, Richard, that your course of instruction is finished. I assure you the same methods that produced the perfect pupil will not be spared to make the ideal husband. In the next few weeks, in fact, I think you will have learned to look back with proper shame

on your conduct earlier tonight..." She paused,
and when she spoke again her voice came with the
cold sibilance of controlled anger. "Are you yet
fully aware of the insult comprised in your refusal
of my rights over you? Answer me."

The wretched youth's cheeks were on fire with
shame, "Oh, Harriet, I did not know. But forgive
me! I tried—"

The whip lashed him sharply across the loins,
cutting short his protestations.

"I did not ask you to recall your affront to me!
And bear in mind that I am not interested in your
excuses. No, your pardon will be granted only
when you repair your fault. But we are wasting
time. Put your hands on your knees!"

The next moment the whip wrapped itself
around his loins with a rich and urgent hiss.
Richard screamed and Harriet exhaled a deep luxurious sigh. Then slowly and with all the strength
of her wrist, she struck again and again.

The wretched youth was soon twisting and
swaying on his feet, his breath coming in great
sobs. "Oh Harriet—I beg you—but I cannot...can-
not—"

"Ah, we shall see!" The whip fell again, directed
this time at the tenderest flesh of his thighs.
"Come now—we shall see..."

And all at once the weeping youth was aware of
a development over which he had no conscious
control. The next moment, with a feeling of blissful incredulity, he felt a mysterious vigor coursing
through his hips and causing his member to
waken—and as he did so his eyes were caught by
the reflection in the great mirror opposite him.
Panting with a newly generated excitement, he saw
the tall caped figure, its bare arm raised in the clas-

sic gesture of correction above the nude cowering body that, for an instant, no longer seemed to be his own. Fired by the vision, with a wild ecstasy, a whole-hearted delight, he saw the whip cutting into the quivering flesh of this impersonal body.

"Ah! Yes, yes!" he cried. "Again—again!"

Once, twice more, the lash wrapped around his thighs. His senses in a delicious chaos, his brain reeling, he was aware of Harriet throwing aside the whip. He saw her cape fall to her feet—and then he was clasped in her bare arms and being borne in triumph to the bed which received them both in its soft depths.

She took him like a goddess or a savage queen, her back arched, her breasts with erected nipples thrust out, the splendid hips pulsating with urgent, imperious motion. Her vulva gripped him like the oiled fist of a wrestler, searching and clapping, importuning the smooth bulb throughout its enforced passage. It was freed, for a moment, from the stringent embrace of the frothing lips, to rub the fleshy finger of her clitoris before being engulfed again up to the spongy cavern of the womb. She drove him further in with an expert stroke of her loins. Then she paused, holding it captive while she ground her buttocks over it with luxurious and leisurely greed.

As she smiled down at him in triumph the arch of her brows was lifted slightly, lengthening the fine curve of her eyes, which were like two shining bowls filled with a cold dry light. "Ah, this is how I like you!" she cried. And leaning forward she took his face in her hands, panting, "A boy—to be whipped and enjoyed, again and again..."

All at once, she began to groan, as if in the act of defecation. She let her breasts fall slowly on his.

Her movements shortened, became more violent, concentrated and her spine stiffened as if in agony. Deep lines sprang out along her thighs, her sides, and her neck. She was shaken by a series of convulsions spreading in a double wave from her loins and prolonging itself to the limits of her frame, as if winding her whole body into the central shuddering ecstasy of the womb.

He achieved his orgasm at the same moment, his sperm jetting weakly into her with the concurrent spasms of his captured and subservient member.

Later, happy and relaxed, he lay on his back, his head turned sideways on the pillow so he could see Harriet's face beside him, and the pure profile it presented. Her dark eyelids drooped over her eyes, but she was not sleeping. Rather, the intent dreamy expression of her flushed face, the pouting contours of her soft mouth, bespoke her pursuit of some further and persistent sensual reverie.

No longer inclined for sleep, he passionately devoured the lines of the beautiful face—the low, classic brow, the short, cruel upper lip, the heavy, voluptuously carved chin and throat. His eye travelled lower and dwelt with livelier admiration on the curve and swell of the naked breasts, whose exposed nipples raised themselves almost within reach of his lips. He drew a deep breath. Never had she seemed more lovely, more desirable, than at this moment when his desire had just exhausted itself...

After a while his eyes grew dim with voluptuousness, and a quiver went through him. His hand, as if acting independently of his will, passed over her thighs and sought her vulva in a burning caress. Turning his head to seek her lips, he found her warm mouth awaiting him. There was a look of renewed expectation, of fresh desire, on her smiling face. He pressed his body against hers feverishly, waiting for his flesh to echo the excitement of his brain. It was not until almost a minute had gone by that he understood what he wished.

Harriet, already stirred by her reveries and the unequivocal caress of his hand, lay awaiting the further and final assuagement of her desire. It was then that she experienced her most intense emotion. When she saw his glowing beautiful face approach hers with a smiling expression of appeal, she heard him asking in low and passionate tones for the boon he now craved with every nerve in his body.

Her eyes closed for an instant in ecstasy. Then, springing to her knees with a single sinuous movement, she reached for the instrument of correction, uttering a glad and savage cry.

Richard was sleeping now, his breath coming with the deep regularity of content and fatigue. Harriet, at last enjoying the bliss of absolute satiety, lay beside him, herself feeling the delicious approach of sleep.

She smiled in the semi-darkness. The promised goal had been reached, her cup full at last. She enjoyed the entire possession and control of the man she loved with all that mixture of tenderness and cruelty that marked her nature. He was indeed, she thought, such as she had made him: a creature dependent on her, body and soul, the plaything of her humors and caprice, the helpless, beloved and obedient instrument of her desires. A vision of the future unrolled itself before her in a sudden blaze of beauty—the vision of a husband whose devotion would never weaken, whose disposition would keep him her willing slave forever.

She breathed deeply, luxuriously. Not for her, she knew, the fate of so many women, not the experience of neglect and indifference, the cooling of a husband's love. Not for her, as the years went by and her beauty waned, the heartbreak and dismay of the woman dependent on her fading physical charms, on artifice and dissimulation, for the satisfaction of her body and the return of affection. Not for her the affront of a pretended admiration nor the pangs of jealousy! She had taken her measures, her patience had its reward, and her prey was safe at last. The man she loved would never falter in his adoration or respect. He could never escape...

Her eyes closed gently, slowly. Happiness flowed over her in a soft wave, lulling her like bodily weariness. As she drifted into slumber her hand reached out involuntarily to the bedside table and touched the whip as if for an assurance, caressing for an instant this symbol of her victory, this talisman of her present joy, this guarantee of her felicity and satisfaction in all the years to come.

Free GIFT

ROSEBUD BOOKS

THE ROSEBUD READER

Rosebud Books—the hottest-selling line of lesbian erotica available—here collects the very best of the best. Rosebud has contributed greatly to the burgeoning genre of lesbian erotica—to the point that authors like Lindsay Welsh, Aarona Griffin and Valentina Cilescu are among the hottest and most closely watched names in lesbian and gay publishing. Here are the finest moments from Rosebud's contemporary classics. $5.95/319-8

LOVECHILD
GAG

From New York's thriving poetry scene comes this explosive volume of work from one of the bravest, most cutting young writers you'll ever encounter. The poems in *Gag* take on American hypocrisy with uncommon energy, and announce Lovechild as a writer of unique and unforgettable rage. $5.95/369-4

ALISON TYLER
THE BLUE ROSE

The tale of a modern sorority—fashioned after a Victorian girls' school. Ignited to the heights of passion by erotic tales of the Victorian age, a group of lusty young women are encouraged to act out their forbidden fantasies—all under the tutelage of Mistresses Emily and Justine, two avid practitioners of hard-core discipline! $5.95/335-X

ELIZABETH OLIVER

THE SM MURDER: Murder at Roman Hill

Intrepid lesbian P.I.s Leslie Patrick and Robin Penny take on a really hot case: the murder of the notorious Felicia Roman..The circumstances of the crime lead the pair on an excursion through the leatherdyke underground, where motives—and desires—run deep. But as Leslie and Robin soon find, every woman harbors her own closely guarded secret.... $5.95/353-8

PAGAN DREAMS

Cassidy and Samantha plan a vacation at a secluded bed-and-breakfast, hoping for a little personal time alone. Their hostess, however, has different plans. The lovers are plunged into a world of dungeons and pagan rites, as the merciless Anastasia steals Samantha for her own. B&B—B&D-style! $5.95/295-7

SUSAN ANDERS

CITY OF WOMEN

A collection of stories dedicated to women and the passions that draw them together. Designed strictly for the sensual pleasure of women, Anders' tales are set to ignite flames of passion from coast to coast. The residents of *City of Women* hold the key to even the most forbidden fantasies. $5.95/375-9

PINK CHAMPAGNE

Tasty, torrid tales of butch/femme couplings—from a writer more than capable of describing the special fire ignited when opposites collide. Tough as nails or soft as silk, these women seek out their antitheses, intent on working out the details of their own personal theory of difference. $5.95/282-5

LAVENDER ROSE
Anonymous

A classic collection of lesbian literature: From the writings of Sappho, Queen of the island Lesbos, to the turn-of-the-century *Black Book of Lesbianism*; from *Tips to Maidens* to *Crimson Hairs*, a recent lesbian saga—here are the great but little-known lesbian writings and revelations. $4.95/208-6

ROSEBUD BOOKS

EDITED BY LAURA ANTONIOU

LEATHERWOMEN II

A follow-up volume to the popular and controversial *Leatherwomen*. Laura Antoniou turns an editor's discerning eye to the writing of women on the edge—resulting in a collection sure to ignite libidinal flames. Leave taboos behind—because these Leatherwomen know no limits.... $4.95/229-9

LEATHERWOMEN

These fantasies, from the pens of new or emerging authors, break every rule imposed on women's fantasies. The hottest stories from some of today's newest and most outrageous writers make this an unforgettable exploration of the female libido. $4.95/3095-4

LESLIE CAMERON

THE WHISPER OF FANS

"Just looking into her eyes, she felt that she knew a lot about this woman. She could see strength, boldness, a fresh sense of aliveness that rocked her to the core. In turn she felt open, revealed under the woman's gaze—all her secrets already told. No need of shame or artifice...." $5.95/259-0

AARONA GRIFFIN

PASSAGE AND OTHER STORIES

An S/M romance. Lovely Nina is frightened by her lesbian passions until she finds herself infatuated with a woman she spots at a local café. One night Nina follows her and finds herself enmeshed in an endless maze leading to a world where women test the edges of sexuality and power. $4.95/3057-1

VALENTINA CILESCU

THE ROSEBUD SUTRA

"Women are hardly ever known in their true light, though they may love others, or become indifferent towards them, may give them delight, or abandon them, or may extract from them all the wealth that they possess." So says *The Rosebud Sutra*—a volume promising women's inner secrets. One woman learns to use these secrets in a quest for pleasure with a succession of lady loves.... $4.95/242-6

THE HAVEN

J craves domination, and her perverse appetites lead her to the Haven: the isolated sanctuary Ros and Annie call home. Soon J forces her way into the couple's world, bringing unspeakable lust and cruelty into their lives. The Dominatrix Who Came to Dinner! $4.95/165-9

MISTRESS MINE

Sophia Cranleigh sits in prison, accused of authoring the "obscene" *Mistress Mine*. For Sophia has led no ordinary life, but has slaved and suffered—deliciously—under the hand of the notorious Mistress Malin. How long had she languished under the dominance of this incredible beauty? $4.95/109-8

LINDSAY WELSH

ROMANTIC ENCOUNTERS

Beautiful Julie, the most powerful editor of romance novels in the industry, spends her days igniting women's passions through books—and her nights fulfilling those needs with a variety of lovers. Julie's two worlds come together with the type of bodice-ripping Harlequin could never imagine! $5.95/359-7

THE BEST OF LINDSAY WELSH

A collection of this popular writer's best work. This author was one of Rosebud's early bestsellers, and remains highly popular. A sampler set to introduce some of the hottest lesbian erotica to a wider audience. $5.95/368-6

RHINOCEROS BOOKS

DAVID MELTZER

UNDER

The author of *The Agency Trilogy* and *Orf* returns with another glimpse of Things to Come. *Under* concerns a sex professional, whose life at the bottom of the social heap is, nevertheless, filled with incident. Other than numerous surgeries designed to increase his physical allure, he is faced with an establishment intent on using any body for unimaginable genetic experiments. The extremes of his world force this cyber-gigolo underground—where even more bizarre cultures await.... $6.95/290-6

ORF

He is the ultimate musician-hero—the idol of thousands, the fevered dream of many more. And like many musicians before him, he is misunderstood, misused—and totally out of control. Every last drop of feeling is squeezed from a modern-day troubadour and his lady love. $6.95/110-1

EDITED BY AMARANTHA KNIGHT

FLESH FANTASTIC

Humans have long toyed with the idea of "playing God": creating life from nothingness, bringing Life to the inanimate. Now Amarantha Knight, author of the "Darker Passions" series of erotic horror novels, collects stories exploring not only the allure of Creation, but the lust that follows.... One of our most shocking and sexy anthologies. $6.95/352-X

GARY BOWEN

DIARY OF A VAMPIRE

"Gifted with a darkly sensual vision and a fresh voice, [Bowen] is a writer to watch out for." —Cecilia Tan

The chilling, arousing, and ultimately moving memoirs of an undead—but all too human—soul. Bowen's Rafael, a red-blooded male with an insatiable hunger for same, is the perfect antidote to the effete malcontents haunting bookstores today. *Diary of a Vampire* marks the emergence of a bold and brilliant vision, firmly rooted in past *and* present. $6.95/331-7

RENE MAIZEROY

FLESHLY ATTRACTIONS

Lucien Hardanges was the son of the wantonly beautiful actress, Marie-Rose Hardanges. When she decides to let a "friend" introduce her son to the pleasures of love, Marie-Rose could not have foretold the erotic excesses that would lead to her own ruin and that of her cherished son. $6.95/299-X

EDITED BY LAURA ANTONIOU

NO OTHER TRIBUTE

A collection of stories sure to challenge Political Correctness in a way few have before, with tales of women kept in bondage to their lovers by their deepest passions. Love pushes these women beyond acceptable limits, rendering them helpless to deny the men and women they adore. A companion volume to *By Her Subdued*. $6.95/294-9

SOME WOMEN

Over forty essays written by women actively involved in consensual dominance and submission. Professional mistresses, lifestyle leatherdykes, whipmakers, titleholders—women from every conceivable walk of life lay bare their true feelings about about issues as explosive as feminism, abuse, pleasures and public image. $6.95/300-7

RHINOCEROS BOOKS

BY HER SUBDUED

Stories of women who get what they want. The tales in this collection all involve women in control—of their lives, their loves, their men. So much in control, in fact, that they can remorselessly break rules to become the powerful goddesses of the men who sacrifice all to worship at their feet. Woman Power with a vengeance! $6.95/281-7

JEAN STINE

SEASON OF THE WITCH

"A future in which it is technically possible to transfer the total mind... of a rapist killer into the brain dead but physically living body of his female victim. Remarkable for intense psychological technique. There is eroticism but it is necessary to mark the differences between the sexes and the subtle altering of a man into a woman." —The Science Fiction Critic $6.95/268-X

JOHN WARREN

THE TORQUEMADA KILLER

Detective Eva Hernandez has finally gotten her first "big case": a string of vicious murders taking place within New York's SM community. Piece by piece, Eva assembles the evidence, revealing a picture of a world misunderstood and under attack—and gradually comes to understand her own place within it. A hot, edge-of-the-seat thriller from the author of *The Loving Dominant*—and an exciting insider's perspective on "the scene." $6.95/367-8

THE LOVING DOMINANT

Everything you need to know about an infamous sexual variation—and an unspoken type of love. Mentor—a longtime player in the dominance/submission scene—guides readers through this world and reveals the too-often hidden basis of the D/S relationship: care, trust and love. $6.95/218-3

GRANT ANTREWS

SUBMISSIONS

Once again, Antrews portrays the very special elements of the dominant/submissive relationship…with restraint—this time with the story of a lonely man, a winning lottery ticket, and a demanding dominatrix. One of erotica's most discerning writers. $6.95/207-8

MY DARLING DOMINATRIX

When a man and a woman fall in love it's supposed to be simple, uncomplicated, easy—unless that woman happens to be a dominatrix. Curiosity gives way to unblushing desire in this story of one man's awakening to the joys to be experienced as the willing slave of a powerful woman. $6.95/3055-5

LAURA ANTONIOU WRITING AS "SARA ADAMSON"

THE TRAINER

The long-awaited conclusion of Adamson's stunning Marketplace Trilogy! The ultimate underground sexual realm includes not only willing slaves, but the exquisite trainers who take submissives firmly in hand. And it is now the time for these mentors to divulge their own secrets—the desires that led them to become the ultimate figures of authority. $6.95/249-3

THE SLAVE

The second volume in the "Marketplace" trilogy. *The Slave* covers the experience of one exceptionally talented submissive who longs to join the ranks of those who have proven themselves worthy of entry into the Marketplace. But the price, while delicious, is staggeringly high…. Adamson's plot thickens, as her trilogy moves to a conclusion in *The Trainer*. $6.95/173-X

RHINOCEROS BOOKS

THE MARKETPLACE

"Merchandise does not come easily to the Marketplace.... They haunt the clubs and the organizations.... Some of them are so ripe that they intimidate the poseurs, the weekend sadists and the furtive dilettantes who are so endemic to that world. And they never stop asking where we may be found...." $6.95/3096-2

THE CATALYST

After viewing a controversial, explicitly kinky film full of images of bondage and submission, several audience members find themselves deeply moved by the erotic suggestions they've seen on the screen. "Sara Adamson"'s sensational debut volume! $5.95/328-7

DAVID AARON CLARK

SISTER RADIANCE

A chronicle of obsession, rife with Clark's trademark vivisections of contemporary desires, sacred and profane. The vicissitudes of lust and romance are examined against a backdrop of urban decay and shallow fashionability in this testament to the allure—and inevitability—of the forbidden. $6.95/215-9

THE WET FOREVER

The story of Janus and Madchen, a small-time hood and a beautiful sex worker, *The Wet Forever* examines themes of loyalty, sacrifice, redemption and obsession amidst Manhattan's sex parlors and underground S/M clubs. Its combination of sex and suspense led Terence Sellers to proclaim it "evocative and poetic." $6.95/117-9

ALICE JOANOU

BLACK TONGUE

"Joanou has created a series of sumptuous, brooding, dark visions of sexual obsession and is undoubtedly a name to look out for in the future."
                                                            —*Redeemer*

Another seductive book of dreams from the author of the acclaimed *Tourniquet*. Exploring lust at its most florid and unsparing, *Black Tongue* is a trove of baroque fantasies—each redolent of the forbidden. Joanou creates some of erotica's most mesmerizing and unforgettable characters. A critical favorite. $6.95/258-2

TOURNIQUET

A heady collection of stories and effusions from the pen of one our dazzling young writers. Strange tales abound, from the story of the mysterious and cruel Cybele, to an encounter with the sadistic entertainment of a bizarre after-hours cafe. A sumptuous feast for all the senses.. $6.95/3060-1

CANNIBAL FLOWER

"She is waiting in her darkened bedroom, as she has waited throughout history, to seduce the men who are foolish enough to be blinded by her irresistible charms....She is the goddess of sexuality, and *Cannibal Flower* is her haunting siren song."—Michael Perkins $4.95/72-6

MICHAEL PERKINS

EVIL COMPANIONS

Set in New York City during the tumultuous waning years of the Sixties, *Evil Companions* has been hailed as "a frightening classic." A young couple explores the nether reaches of the erotic unconscious in a shocking confrontation with the extremes of passion. With a new introduction by science fiction legend Samuel R. Delany. $6.95/3067-9

RHINOCEROS BOOKS

AN ANTHOLOGY OF CLASSIC ANONYMOUS EROTIC WRITING

Michael Perkins, acclaimed authority on erotic literature, has collected the very best passages from the world's erotic writing—especially for Rhinoceros readers. "Anonymous" is one of the most infamous bylines in publishing history—and these steamy excerpts show why! $6.95/140-3

THE SECRET RECORD: Modern Erotic Literature

Michael Perkins, a renowned author and critic of sexually explicit fiction, surveys the field with authority and unique insight. Updated and revised to include the latest trends, tastes, and developments in this misunderstood and maligned genre. An important volume for every erotic reader and fan of high quality adult fiction. $6.95/3039-3

HELEN HENLEY

ENTER WITH TRUMPETS

Helen Henley was told that woman just don't write about sex—much less the taboos she was so interested in exploring. So Henley did it alone, flying in the face of "tradition" by producing *Enter With Trumpets*, a touching tale of arousal and devotion in one couple's kinky relationship. $6.95/197-7

PHILIP JOSE FARMER

FLESH

Space Commander Stagg explored the galaxies for 800 years. Upon his return, the hero Stagg is made the centerpiece of an incredible public ritual—one that will repeatedly take him to the heights of ecstasy, and inexorably drag him toward the depths of hell. $6.95/303-1

A FEAST UNKNOWN

"Sprawling, brawling, shocking, suspenseful, hilarious…"
—Theodore Sturgeon

Farmer's supreme anti-hero returns. *A Feast Unknown* begins in 1968, with Lord Grandrith's stunning statement: "I was conceived and born in 1888." Slowly, Lord Grandrith—armed with the belief that he is the son of Jack the Ripper—tells the story of his remarkable and unbridled life. Beginning with his discovery of the secret of immortality, Grandrith's tale proves him no raving lunatic—but something far more bizarre…. $6.95/276-0

THE IMAGE OF THE BEAST

Herald Childe has seen Hell, glimpsed its horror in an act of sexual mutilation. Childe must now find and destroy an inhuman predator through the streets of a polluted and decadent Los Angeles of the future. One clue after another leads Childe to an inescapable realization about the nature of sex and evil…. $6.95/166-7

SAMUEL R. DELANY

EQUINOX

The *Scorpion* has sailed the seas in a quest for every possible pleasure. Her crew is a collection of the young, the twisted, the insatiable. A drifter comes into their midst, and is taken on a fantastic journey to the darkest, most dangerous sexual extremes—until he is finally a victim to their boundless appetites. $6.95/157-8

DANIEL VIAN

ILLUSIONS

Two tales of danger and desire in Berlin on the eve of WWII. From private homes to lurid cafés, passion is exposed and explored in stark contrast to the brutal violence of the time. A singularly arousing volume. $6.95/3074-1